THE COVENANT
OF
GLASS

Glen Carty

Dedication

"For the voices kept in jars... the quiet burden of those who carry their shame alone.

...and the rivers that refuse to be silenced, roaring for the courage of the ones who finally break the glass."

"River nuh stop run."

(The river never stops flowing; time and truth continue regardless of what we do.)
— Jamaican Proverb

"Moon a run, but day ketch im."

(Secrets may travel in the dark, but the light always overtakes them.)
— Jamaican Proverb

TABLE OF CONTENTS

PART 1

GLEN CARTY

CHAPTER 1

The Woman in the Water

They say the Peace River wears two faces.

By day it is open and ordinary: women knee-deep at the bank, slapping wet cloth against stone; the echoes carrying like a single heartbeat through the valley of Wataside. Children wade in the shallows, chasing minnows with cupped hands, squealing when the slick bodies slide away. The air is busy with chatter—who is ill, who is expecting, who borrowed and never returned. By day, the river belongs to the village.

But when dusk creeps in, the river sheds its common skin.

The women tie their headcloths and go, the children are called in with sharp voices, and the dogs creep under the steps. The surface darkens, thick as oil; the current keeps its secrets close. By night, the river belongs to itself.

It was at that hour Zion slipped from his mother's yard.

He was a small, quiet twelve-year-old who noticed a lot but spoke very little. He walked barefoot and silent on the dusty ground, as if the tamarind tree roots whispered that he shouldn't be there. He told himself he was only wandering, only walking to feel the coolness coming up from the water. But the pull had no words. It was the same pull that draws a moth to flame, or a stone to the bottom of a well.

At the bend where the almond tree leaned crooked across the stream, he stopped.

The air here was different. It was heavy. It smelled of ancient mud and iron.

A woman was in the river.

She stood waist-deep, her back to him. She didn't move like a bather. She moved with a terrifying, fluid slowness, as if the water were part of her body. Her arms lifted, combing the current as if it were strands of silver hair, and every ripple bowed to her command.

Zion crouched among the roots, paralyzed. This was not a duppy. This was something older.

Then it came—the voice.

It didn't come from the river. It came from the marrow of his bones.

Don't be afraid, Zion. Come.

His heart stumbled. No one had spoken, yet the words had weight.

She turned.

She didn't have a human face—not exactly. In the half-light, her features seemed to shift like foam on water. Her eyes were hollows of dark liquid, indifferent and vast. It was not the look of a stranger startled by a child; it was the look of a landlord inspecting a tenant.

She beckoned with one dripping hand.

He slid from the roots, half crawling, half stumbling. His chest rose in short, sharp breaths. Sense told him to run, yet awe pinned him where he stood. The murmur of the stream thickened, carrying more than sound—as if a thousand voices lay hidden beneath the surface, screaming to be let out.

At the edge of the bank, he saw her hand open.

In her palm rested a stone. It was oval, smooth, and dark as midnight.

She beckoned with one dripping hand... Here, she said inside him. Take the weight. I can go no further, but you must.

Zion reached out. His fingers brushed the cold, wet surface.

As soon as he took it, his arm yanked down. The Stone was impossibly heavy. It hummed—not sound but vibration, a low thrumming bass note that rattled his teeth.

It is an anchor, she whispered, the words blooming like a bruise in his mind. It holds steady what must not be let loose.

Zion took it with both hands, trembling, unable to let go.

Go now. She turned her back, swaying once more to comb the current. And remember—when a voice you cannot see calls your name, answer only once. After that, you make them hungry.

Zion backed away, The Stone burning cold in his fist. The ripples curled outward though she did not move. He stumbled homeward, skin prickling with the sense of carrying a mountain in his pocket.

THE COVENANT OF GLASS

He slipped through the door just as the lamplight took the chill off the little front room.

His mother, Caro, sat with her elbows on her knees and her headscarf loosened; the day's burdens had finally settled into a heavy silence. She lifted her eyes at the scrape of Zion's heel on the threshold. She saw at once what a stranger would have missed: wet cuffs clinging to his skinny ankles, the faint smell of river grass on his skin, and the way his left hand clutched his pocket as if holding it shut against a gale.

"Wash your hands," she said, though his hands were clean.

She did not ask where he had been. She did not ask what had pulled him out at that hour. Silence can be both a scolding and a shelter. There are some questions a mother will not ask because she fears the answers they might reveal.

Zion ate lightly, as if he had forgotten how to be hungry. He lay down early with his hand in his pocket. The Stone was against his skin, cold and quiet, an anchor pulling him toward sleep.

~ ~ ~

Sleep did not arrive; it fell on him like a curtain. In that dark, a voice came not creeping but striding.

Doorway, it said, dragging the word like a chain.

A figure limped toward him across a floor he could not see. Cloth wrapped the body in strips; the head was bowed. The tap of a staff counted the distance: once, twice, three times. When the figure raised its face, there was only one eye, dull as cold ash. The lid over the other was folded down and bandaged. The smell of river weed came off him in a low tide reek.

Doorway, the voice said again, pleased the way a thirsty man is pleased to find a cup. You will keep the path. You will open when it is time.

Zion tried to speak but found his tongue stuck to the roof of his mouth. He tried to step back, but the dream held him like molasses. The one-eyed man leaned close. The staff's knotted head pressed a mark into Zion's sternum without touching him. The Stone in his palm burned in reply.

The door is sealed, the voice murmured, not asking, stating. The weight is warm in your hand. The house has many rooms. We will go one by one until it is built again.

The bandaged eye seemed to glow behind the cloth, an ember trying to breathe itself into flame.

Zion forced a whisper through the dry crack of his lips. "Who… who are you?"

The mouth twisted as though at a joke told twice.

You will remember me when they speak my name, said the voice. And when you answer, I will be waiting.

The staff tapped once more, and the tap echoed like a hammer in an empty chapel. Zion woke biting his own tongue, a trickle of blood and the taste of iron blooming in his mouth.

From the other side of the room his mother's breathing came steady as tide. She had heard nothing and everything, the way mothers do.

Chapter 2
The Broken Seal

Light came thin and gray. Zion washed his face as boys do—quick, careless—and wiped the water away with the edge of his shirt.

Zion entered the kitchen when Caro, already at the pot, said without turning, "Pass me the tin." She meant the one with lard, the one she stowed under the shelf because rats fancied the smell.

He fetched it, but when his mouth opened to say "here", something else flowed out.

It wasn't his voice. It was cold. It was flat. It was the voice of a Prosecutor reading a verdict.

"Behind the book. Under the cloth. Folded once. The letter the pastor keeps. The one with her name on it. The edge torn where he read it

too many times. Kept with another, meant for Elias—listing his shame."

He was as surprised to hear the words as his mother was to receive them. The ladle paused mid-stir. The smell of fried dumplings and boiling green banana hung in the small room like a cover thrown over a birdcage.

"What foolishness you talking?" Caro asked softly, but her voice was firm and had no slack in it. Her eyes flicked through the open doorway to the shelf in the front room where the family Bible lay—then away, as if the name itself might slip out. She did not move toward it. She turned the fire instead, propping a piece of wood in the fire pit beside the stove, letting the question burn down in the ash.

Zion blinked. He didn't remember choosing the words. He felt as if he had come back to his body after someone else had worn it to do an errand.

He took the tin down and set it on the table. His hand shook and he hid the shake in his pocket, pressing The Stone to keep it still. The heat had faded, but a faint hum remained, like the sound a conch shell keeps after it has been lifted from the ear.

They ate. The birds seemed unusually loud in the mango tree. When Zion stood to go, Caro reached out, then pulled her hand back.

"If anyone ask you anything," she said, "answer once."

"Yes, Ma," Zion said. "But... why?"

Caro stilled. Her brow furrowed, searching backward. "Old folks used to say it when I was a girl. Never made much sense to me. Just... answer once to let them know you heard them. After that..." She let the words trail off, as though even remembering them put a stone in her chest. "...after that, it's like you're giving them permission."

~ ~ ~

Villages are built of timber, zinc, stone, and talk. Wataside, perched on the edge of the Peace River, was no different.

A thing spoken in one yard at sunrise will sit on eleven verandas by noon. Sister Etta at the standpipe heard first—not about the letter itself, but the thing the boy had said. She pressed her palm to Auntie Myra's wrist and leaned in close.

"Miss Caro boy. Zion. Early this very morning."

"And who tell you so?"

"My own eye. I was passing by and hear the tail of it."

"Cho… Tail always longer than body, Etta."

They laughed, but their laughter was thin. Then Etta lowered her voice. "You remember that man… the one with —? The boy call his name."

Myra did not speak. She drew her finger across her eyelid slowly, a sign more than a word. Her glance darted over her shoulder before she muttered, low enough only Etta heard: "Pastor know more 'bout him than he ever admit. Mark my words."

Before Etta could answer, a ball skittered into their skirts, making them both jump. Patch, the village mongrel, bounded after it, tail high, tongue lolling, scattering the tension. The women hissed and swatted at the dog as he nosed the ball back to the giggling children.

"Go play somewhere else—and take that dog with you!" one mother called, shooing them down the lane. Patch trotted after them, ears perked, as if nothing in the world was heavier than a game.

By the time Pastor Williams heard, the letter itself felt heavier in his hand than paper has any right to feel. He stood alone in the church's side room, the torn edge scraping his thumb. He did not read it again. He slid it back under the cloth behind the book and closed the door.

~ ~ ~

By evening, one story traveled faster than the rest: the boy who spoke grown-folk secrets. That tale belonged to kitchens, where women stirred pots, and to verandas, where men remembered other evenings long ago when jars had turned up in strange places—under steps, behind trunks, inside huts no one claimed.

They did not say obeah loudly; some words call themselves if shouted.

"You remember yesterday when we see Miss Caro boy heading to the river? Suppose him free something?" a girl whispered.

Her friend clapped her hands over her ears, humming until the thought went quiet.

THE COVENANT OF GLASS

Two names kept surfacing and sinking like fish: Elias. Marcia Brown. People had stories ready. Some said she'd gone to Kingston. Some said the Peace River had taken her on a blue day—a cloudless day when the water ran deceptively wild. And some said she and the obeah man, Elias, killed her husband.

No one said which tale they believed, but a muscle twitched beneath every jaw whenever Marcia or Elias's name was spoken.

That night, Pastor Williams prayed long, his knuckles white as stone. When he opened his eyes, he saw the church window holding the river's reflection, as if the water itself had come to press its face against the glass.

~ ~ ~

Deep in the night, Zion stirred and lay listening. The house ticked as wood settles after heat. A lizard clicked in the rafters. The Stone was a cool moon in his palm.

His name floated through the dark.

"Zion..."

He answered before he thought, a whisper hardly louder than his breath.

Silence. Then again, closer—drawn-out, not hungry, but fluid, like water lapping against a bank.

"Zion…"

The voice was familiar. It was the Lady. His lips parted reflexively to answer, but he remembered her words: When a voice you cannot see calls your name, answer only once.

His throat closed. He clutched The Stone until it pressed hard against his palm, forcing himself to stay silent, just in case.

His mother shifted on her bed, sighing in her sleep. Zion lay frozen, the echo of the call curling in his ears.

Then another name rose into the room. It wasn't his, and it wasn't hers. It was detached, muffled as if spoken underwater—not a summons, just a fact floating up from the deep, heavy with an old weight:

"Marcia Brown."

The words did not come from his mouth, yet they hovered in the air like steam escaping a kettle.

THE COVENANT OF GLASS

"She's coming home," Zion whispered, though he did not know why he said it, and the sentence landed in the dark with a soft weight, like a bird that had flown a long way and found the right branch at last.

~ ~ ~

The village did not sleep in full. A few doors down, the light in Pastor Williams's window was still a bright, hard square, chasing back the dark. And out under the mango tree that shaded the community path, Patch lay sprawled.

He was bored. The noise had been exciting earlier—the women clustered, the men arguing with their hands—but now the talking had faded into the usual night sounds. Patch lifted his head, blinked once at the lamplight, and sighed, resting his chin back down on his front paws. He was asleep before his tail settled.

Then, the name surfaced.

Not shouted, not whispered, but traveling on the air like an electric current—a name that had been a silent tombstone for twenty years.

Marcia Brown.

Patch's ears snapped up. He heard the name at the very moment Zion heard it too. He watched Zion's house without blinking. The ridge along his spine lifted one hair at a time, a slow brush drawn backward. A growl rippled through his ribs but didn't break. He saw his trusted friend, Zion, leave the house and take the trail toward the river.

The friendly dog that chased minnows by day was gone. He barked once—a panicked, desolate sound that cut the silence—then turned and ran, low to the ground. He did not run toward Zion; he simply ran away, as if a line had been crossed that no dog should stand on.

~ ~ ~

Zion walked alone, his hand clenched around The Stone in his pocket, his legs carrying him without his asking. He stepped into the dark yard, an unseen force guiding him toward the water.

Somewhere ahead, a bottle clinked once against a root. On the path, something heavy dragged and rattled in the dust. The Peace River did not answer, but the ripples widened all the same.

18

THE COVENANT OF GLASS

The almond tree bent crooked over the bend, its branches clawing at the stars. The bank smelled of wet earth turned sour in the night air, and the mist that curled above the water shone faintly in the moonlight. His heel struck a lump beneath the slick mud. He crouched and scraped it free.

A jar rose into his hands, its glass dim and streaked, the cork blackened and waxed shut. In the silver wash of the moon it looked more stone than glass, heavy and old, as if it had been buried there to keep the dark itself sealed.

Something pale flickered inside, but faintly, as if even the glow feared the night.

His breath shortened. The Stone in his pocket turned ice cold—a sharp, freezing warning against his leg. He should have put it back. He told himself so.

But the jar wasn't silent. A low, rhythmic thrumming came from the glass, a vibration of pure want that pulled at his fingers. Curiosity is the first hand that opens most doors, but hunger is the second.

He pressed his thumb against the wax, meeting the cold, stubborn resistance of the years. When it held fast, he wedged the tip of a stick beneath the blackened rim and twisted. The seal surrendered with a soft, wet sigh—a suction breaking, a lung inhaling—and in that single, irreversible moment, the heavy silence of the valley shattered. The world changed.

Not a wind—but a pressure, as if everything around him drew in one long breath and forgot how to release it. The trees along the bank shivered without moving. The river heaved once, a tug felt deep in his bones. Then came the sound: thin, muffled, aching—a child's cry heard through water, as if life itself had tried to be born and been smothered.

Zion stumbled back. The jar slipped from his hands and struck a stone. It did not shatter, but its silence was broken. A shape without shape—a breath without lungs—leapt free and was gone.

His knees sank into the mud. He pressed both hands against The Stone in his pocket as if it could cork what he had unleashed. It burned in his grip, humming like a heart not his own. The cry faded, but the air did not ease.

Zion fled, The Stone burning in his fist. Behind him, the river kept its secrets, but something had slipped loose.

CHAPTER 3
Marcia's Return

The night had been like a fist closing tight around the village secrets. When the sun finally rose over Wataside, it did so with a brutal, exposing clarity.

The air felt thin. The chatter of the morning birds was notably absent, and the dust motes dancing in the light seemed to carry a static charge.

In the small house, Caro moved like a woman wading through a fog. She fried the dumplings and brewed the tea, performing her routine acts of normalcy as a desperate prayer. She would not meet Zion's eyes. She didn't have to; the boy sat still, the black stone a silent lump in his pocket, radiating a faint, residual heat. He didn't speak the previous morning's foolishness again, but the damage was done.

The Name had been spoken.

By the time the sun had cleared the cane fields, the village was no longer itself. Fear moves faster than gossip. The sound of a frantic, whimpering dog fleeing into the bush had been a far more credible witness than any dream. Every conversation circled back to Zion's whisper and the name of the woman who vanished without a trace.

Zion stepped out into the yard. He found Patch huddled in the shade of the mango tree, where he'd fled the night before.

But the dog was utterly changed.

He was curled tight, tail tucked so far under his belly it seemed to be pulling his spine. His coat looked dull. When Zion called his name—softly, gently—Patch's head snapped up. He whined—a low, pained sound—and scooted backward, pressing his body into the dirt. His eyes darted between Zion and the open road, seeing things that weren't there.

Zion reached out a hand. Patch snapped—not a bite, but a warning click of teeth—and scrambled away under the house.

Zion pulled his hand back. The Stone in his pocket gave a single, heavy throb against his leg.

~ ~ ~

It was late morning when the silence truly broke. It wasn't the sound of an approaching cart or a greeting call; it was the sudden, collective hush that dropped over the marketplace.

Marcia Brown arrived not as a ghost, but as a ruin.

She walked barefoot on the dirt road, stepping out of the heat haze like a figure carved from driftwood. Her clothes were rags, torn and bleached by exposure, and her hair was a mass of white-streaked knots. Her skin was pulled tight over her bones, bearing the mark of two decades spent outside of time.

But the villagers recognized the shape of her jaw, the way she carried her shoulders. It was a proud woman who had been ground down into dust.

Her eyes were the worst. They were not seeing the mango trees, or the houses, or the faces of the people she'd known. They were hollow, fixed on a world only she could perceive.

"Marcia?" Old Auntie Myra was the first to speak, the name barely a breath.

Marcia stopped. She didn't look at Myra. She looked at the ground. Her voice was a dry rasp, like stones scraping together.

"Him never died," she said.

The words carried across the yard without shouting.

"They didn't kill him. Elias was kept."

She lifted her head. Her hollow eyes swept the crowd, landing on Zion, who stood frozen with Caro in their doorway.

"He was kept in river-binding," she rasped. "Waiting for a vessel. The binding is broken now. He is coming, and he has many, many debts to collect."

The shock of her return was a physical thing, but her words were the match that lit the fire. The villagers recoiled. Elias was a shared, buried shame, and Marcia's return meant that shame was now walking the roads.

Zion stepped forward.

He didn't move his lips at first. The air around him thickened, the pressure dropping as if a storm were breaking directly over his head. When he spoke, it wasn't the voice of a child. It was the voice of The Stone. It was the Prosecutor.

"The cane crop," Zion said. His voice rang with a cold authority that froze the blood. "Miss Etta's field. It was not the wind."

Etta let out a thin, terrified squeak.

"It was your husband," Zion intoned, his eyes blank and terrifyingly clear. "Stealing sugar to pay off the debt he made to get you to stay."

Etta's husband went pale, the blood draining from his face. He looked at the ground, convicted without a trial.

Zion did not wait. He turned his gaze to the next target.

"And the child, Auntie Myra."

Myra stumbled backward, clutching her hand to the faded silver ring on her finger.

"The one who wasn't his," Zion said, the words cutting through the humid air. "Sold away to somebody in Kingston for a price when she was five years old."

Myra gasped.

"The silver ring you wear," Zion said mercilessly. "That was the payment. That was the price you took to bury your shame."

Myra burst into furious tears, her grief weaponized by paranoia. She looked at her neighbors—the ones who had always whispered about her vanity—and saw only accusations.

"And you," Zion said, turning to a young woman near the standpipe. "Sister Etta's daughter. You did not work in an office."

The young woman collapsed into the dust before he could finish.

Adultery. Theft. Abandonment.

Zion was stripping the roof off the village. The neighbors didn't look at the boy-prophet; they looked at each other. Decades of forced smiles and quiet neighborliness were shredded in minutes. Every person looked at their neighbor and saw a liar, a thief, or a sinner who had trafficked with the obeah man.

Marcia began to move. She pushed through the stunned crowd, her eyes locked on Zion. She walked with a terrible, singular purpose.

Then Patch exploded.

The dog shot out from under the house, a streak of chaotic fur. He wasn't whimpering anymore. He was barking a confused, frantic challenge. He slammed into Marcia's legs, biting at the rags wrapped around her ankles.

He ignored the villagers. He targeted only Marcia. But it wasn't an attack of aggression; it was the desperate defense of a guard protecting a boundary he didn't understand.

Marcia didn't flinch. She barely registered the dog.

As Patch bit down, she didn't flinch nor kick at him. Instead, a sharp, dry sound split the air—the violent discharge of a static shock.

Crack.

Patch yelped—a sound of acute, human-like pain—and was thrown violently backward, skidding ten feet into the dirt.

He scrambled away, terrified, retreating into the deep shadows between the mango tree roots. He had tried to bite a woman who had been claimed by the darkness, and the claim had not yet totally worn off.

Marcia didn't stop. She walked past the whimpering dog, past the weeping women. As she passed, the sun caught the depths of her hollow eyes.

For a second, Caro saw it too—a violent, involuntary tremor running through the woman's hand, the only sign that the shock had burned her just as badly as it had the dog—before Marcia vanished into the crowd, leaving the ruin of the village in her wake.

CHAPTER 4
The Price of Ambition

It was twenty years ago.

Thomas Williams was not yet "Pastor Williams." He was just Thomas—a young man with too much fire, too much ambition, and a church the size of a storage shed.

His sermons were thunder. His faith was iron. But his congregation refused to grow beyond a scattering of six elderly women and a perpetually sleeping groundskeeper. Every Sunday, looking out at the empty wooden benches, he felt the same gnawing panic: failure. He had a vision of ministry—a soaring wooden sanctuary, a choir that filled the valley of Wataside—but his reality was peeling paint and the sound of crickets drowning out his prayers.

He prayed until his knees bled, but heaven remained silent.

The answer, when it came, walked the earth in the form of Elias.

Williams knew the risk. The Obeah man's compound was secluded, cut off from the village by a sea of whispering cane. Elias was the shadow that Wataside cast. He dealt in spiritual commerce: trading favors, love, and health for strange tokens and unbreakable promises. He was the root of the village's darkest shame, the thing they confessed only in private sickness.

One humid Tuesday, consumed by the vision of the sanctuary he couldn't build, Williams walked the path.

The air around the compound changed. It grew heavy, thick with the scent of unwashed herbs, wet earth, and goat fat. The cane stalks seemed to lean in, listening.

He found Elias hunched over a fire pit, his single eye glinting in the dark like a wet stone.

"The man of God comes to beg," Elias rasped. He didn't look up. "What does the Lord's servant lack that he must seek the Devil's aid?"

Williams felt the lie catch in his throat, but he swallowed it down. "I lack the ability to draw souls to the Word," he said, trying to sound firm. "I need help to build His house."

Elias chuckled. It was a dry, rattling sound, like a snake shedding its skin.

"Souls, you say? I deal in tokens and debt. You want a crowd, Thomas. You want a name."

Elias stood up. He was taller than he looked, unfolded like a mantis.

"The House of God is built on faith," Elias whispered. "The House of Elias is built on desperation."

The bargain was simple. And terrible.

Elias would turn the spiritual current of the valley. He would send the people to the church. He would give Williams the crowds, the resources, and the reverence.

In exchange, Williams had to offer Elias not money, but silence.

"You will be the cork," Elias said. "When the debt collector comes, you will use your voice to keep the village quiet. You will be the guardian of my secret."

Thomas hesitated. He knew, deep down, what this was. It was a spiritual siphon. Every soul that filled his magnificent sanctuary would be fuel for Elias's dark power. He would be building a church on top of a graveyard.

But he looked at his empty hands. He thought of the empty pews.

"I accept," Thomas said.

Elias raised his staff. The head was a knot of dry, gnarled wood wrapped in blackened leather. He pressed it lightly against the center of Thomas's palm.

Hiss.

It wasn't heat. It was a freezing cold burn—a brand of ice that shot up Thomas's arm and lodged in his heart.

"The Lord rewards your ambition," Elias whispered, smiling with his one eye. "Go now. Speak of me no more. Your congregation will grow, but your debt is eternal."

Thomas left the hut, dizzy and sickened. He burned his sermon notes that night. He replaced his messages of suffering with messages of prosperity.

And the people came.

THE COVENANT OF GLASS

~ ~ ~

Twenty years later, the sanctuary was magnificent. The wood soared. The choir filled the valley.

But inside the rectory, the air was stale.

Pastor Williams sat at his desk, the lamp casting long shadows against the wall. His hand—the one Elias had marked—throbbed with a dull, phantom ache.

On the desk in front of him lay a piece of paper. It was yellowed with age, folded once. The edge was torn where he had rubbed it with his thumb a thousand times.

It was a letter he had written to Elias shortly after he first asked Elias to send him a congregation. In it, he begged for release and confessed to selling his soul for greatness and agreeing to aid Elias in his endeavors. A letter he had never had the courage to send.

"Behind the book. Under the cloth. The letter the pastor keeps."

The boy's voice echoed in his head. Zion had described it perfectly. The tear. The fold. The location.

Williams's hands shook. He looked at the window. The reflection of the Peace River pressed against the glass, dark and heavy.

He thought the debt was paid with his silence. He thought Elias was dead, buried in the rumors of the past.

But as he stared at the letter, Pastor Williams realized the truth. The tap of the staff twenty years ago hadn't been a blessing. It had been a down payment.

And now, the landlord was coming to collect the rent.

CHAPTER 5
The Village Ascendant

Pastor Williams arrived in the village center like a thunderhead.

He wore his finest white robes, starched and pressed, the gold cross gleaming on his chest. His face was set in the rigid mask of a man accustomed to authority, but his eyes were darting. The rumors from the morning—the boy speaking secrets, the return of the witch—had soured the air.

He needed a victory. He needed to cut the rot out before it spread to his pews.

He found Zion seated on the steps of the old community hall. The boy was small, barefoot, and unnervingly still. Caro stood beside him, her hand on his shoulder, rigid as an iron rod.

Around them, the village had gathered. They were silent, waiting. They wanted their shepherd to put the world back in order.

Williams didn't approach the boy directly. He commanded the space, lifting his arms wide to encompass the entire crowd.

"We have witnessed the work of disturbers!" his voice boomed, calibrated for the open air. "But God does not allow chaos to reign in His flock! The only power these spirits possess is the power we give them through fear!"

He stepped toward Zion, holding his heavy leather Bible aloft like a shield.

"Boy," he declared, his voice dropping to a sharp, dangerous register. "I command the lying spirit within you to identify itself and release this vessel!"

Zion looked up.

His eyes, usually deep brown and liquid, were momentarily clear and empty. It was the look of a mirror reflecting the sun.

A tremor ran through Williams. A familiar, deep burning cold originated in the palm of his right hand—the spot where

Elias had placed his staff twenty years ago. The sensation was paralyzing.

Then, Zion spoke.

It was the Strange Tongue. The Prosecutor. The voice of The Stone.

"You speak of lies, Thomas?"

The voice coiled around the Pastor's given name, stripping away his title.

"You speak of God's flock," Zion continued, his voice flat and terrifyingly loud. "But you bought the sheep."

The crowd went dead silent.

"You cried in the dirt of the cane field," Zion intoned. "You promised silence for a congregation you could not win. You traded your voice for a full house."

Williams's face drained of color. The burning in his hand intensified, shooting up his arm like a wire pulled tight.

"Silence!" Williams roared, waving the Bible. "I rebuke you!"

Zion didn't flinch. He leaned forward, the prosecutor delivering the final evidence.

"And the child, Thomas. The one you share with Auntie Myra."

The crowd gasped. The sound was a physical wave that struck the Pastor.

"The one sold to Kingston for coin," Zion said mercilessly. "You brokered the deal. You took the fee. You buried the sin in a glass jar with wax, but the wax is melting."

Auntie Myra, standing near the back, let out a sob of pure horror. The villagers turned to look at her, then back at the Pastor. They saw the truth written in his panic. They saw a man who wasn't fighting a demon; he was fighting his own history.

Williams stood immobilized. His elegant words of exorcism died in his throat. He saw his congregation fracturing—not just disappointed, but scandalized. The foundation of their spiritual life had just been exposed as a debt owed to the darkness.

Then, the crowd parted.

They moved not out of respect, but out of fear. Marcia Brown walked through the gap.

She moved with her halting, ruined gait, her hollow eyes fixed on the devastated Pastor.

"Elias is hungry, Thomas," Marcia rasped.

She stopped right in front of him. She was small, frail, a gust of wind away from falling, but she held the Pastor's gaze with the weight of twenty years of torture.

"He uses the boy to speak," Marcia whispered, "but he wants more. He wants to break the binding and enter the boy's soul. He wants a new vessel."

Williams stared at her, his chest heaving. "He... he promised..." Thomas stopped before saying more, staunching the reflex to respond, knowing it would only bury him.

"He promised nothing but debt," Marcia hissed. She stepped closer, lowering her voice so only he could hear. "You want to stop him? You want to be free of the bargain?"

Williams nodded, a barely perceptible motion.

"The jars," Marcia whispered. Her breath smelled of river brine. "They are what he feeds on. You have the influence. You have the hands."

She reached out and touched his robe with a finger that looked like a dry twig. "Gather them, Thomas. Fetch them from the dark."

Williams looked at her, desperation clawing at his eyes. "And then?"

"And then we can defeat him," Marcia urged. "He is getting weak, that's how I escaped."

Williams straightened up. The flush that returned to his face was not the glow of health, but the heat of a new, dangerous ambition. He saw a way out—not just to defeat Elias, but to be the victor. It would be a victory not to be shared; he would be the sole hero of the valley. If he destroyed the vessels, the evidence of his own bargain would be ground into the dirt along with the Obeah man's power. He could frame his own survival as a holy crusade.

"Gather them?" Williams mumbled to himself. "Why?" An idea was taking root and spreading like a weed. "I will smash them all."

He turned to look at Zion. The boy was watching him with those terrible, old eyes, but Williams no longer saw a child; he saw a witness he needed to silence. His fingers, trembling with a sudden, frantic energy, lost their grip.

THE COVENANT OF GLASS

The Bible slipped from his grasp.

It hit the dust with a heavy thud—the most sacred object he possessed, abandoned in the dirt. He didn't pick it up. He didn't even seem to notice it was gone. His mind was already miles away, rehearsing the sermon that would turn his shame into a war.

He turned and walked away, his white robes flapping in the rising wind, moving with the desperate speed of a man who believes he can finally outrun his own shadow.

The Exorcism had failed. The Crusade was about to begin.

CHAPTER 6
The Old Bargain

Marcia Brown had not been born to whispers.

She was born to laughter, to the clatter of iron pots and the rich scent of coconut oil warming on her mother's stove. She had been known in her youth for her bold tongue and her fine cheekbones. Men lingered when she passed; women called her "pretty trouble," and she did not mind. Trouble had its uses.

When she married Leonard Brown, she thought herself fortunate. He was a handsome cane cutter, his shoulders strong, his voice a velvet baritone. He filled her yard with songs of Marley and Alton Ellis, promises of a future stitched in hard work and fidelity.

For a while, the promises held.

Then came the silences. The long absences. The sour smell of white rum on his shirt.

Marcia tried. She cooked the dishes he loved, pressed his shirts sharp, held her tongue when he stumbled home late. But the more she gave, the less of him remained. She woke some nights to find him staring at the ceiling as if another life called to him through the boards. By dawn, his eyes were blank as a field of cane.

The women at the standpipe said what women always say: If a man strays, bind his heart. If his eyes wander, tie them back to you.

Some laughed it off. Some shook their heads. But there were others who whispered of Elias, the old Obeah man in the cane fields. He dealt not in kindness but in contracts. A drop of blood, a strand of hair, a token buried under the bed—he could knot a man's desire so tight he would choke on it.

Marcia listened. And when the nights grew too long, when Leonard's bed grew cold and her womb remained empty, she listened harder.

~ ~ ~

The path to Elias's hut was a road most women walked only once. The cane closed around her shoulders like curtains, the stalks rattling with an unseen wind.

The hut sagged, patched with rusted zinc and boards gone soft with mildew. Smoke lifted through a hole in the roof, smelling not of firewood but of bitter herbs and something rank—animal fat, perhaps, or blood gone old.

Elias sat outside on a low stool, his one eye gleaming like a wet stone.

"The young wife," he rasped, as though he had been expecting her. "Pretty trouble come to bargain."

Her throat closed. She had not spoken her name.

"I want my husband back," she said, forcing her voice steady. "I want him to only love me. I want him tied to me."

Elias smiled without showing teeth. "Love is a costly thing, child. A man's heart is not tied with thread. It is tied with blood. You sure?"

Marcia nodded. "Me sure."

He pricked her palm with a crooked needle and caught the drop in a small glass vial. He whispered over it, words that made the air ripple. Then he gave her a scar, not to heal

44

but to mark—two slashes across the inside of her wrist, thin but deep, that puckered into a pale cross.

"So you will remember the price," he said.

The instructions were simple. She was to bury the vial beneath the bed, and by the next moon Leonard's feet would not carry him anywhere else.

She did as told. And at first, it worked. Leonard stayed home. He lay heavy beside her, his breath warm on her neck. She thought herself blessed.

But blessings curdle.

~ ~ ~

Leonard's love did not soften—it grew—it suffocated.

He followed her to the standpipe, to the market, even to her mother's yard. His voice, once velvet, grew sharp with suspicion. He asked who she spoke to, why she looked this way, why she smiled at that man. He struck her once, then twice.

Worse than the blows was his hunger. It was not love but a gnawing need, bottomless and frantic. He touched her as if trying to climb inside her skin, as if afraid she might vanish if he did not devour her whole.

Marcia went back to Elias, trembling. "I asked for love, not this," she cried.

Elias leaned on his staff, his eye amused. "I gave you what you paid for. His heart is yours. You should have been careful what you asked. Debt does not return to sender."

She begged him to undo it. He laughed. "Undo? You think love is a knot to untie? No. If you want release, you must pay more. Much more."

She fled the hut, her wrist burning where the scar glowed faintly under her skin.

~ ~ ~

Leonard's death by the river should have freed her.

That was what she told herself when they pulled his body from the reeds. He had walked into the water on a blue day, his eyes fixed on something only he could see. But freedom was not a gift Elias gave.

THE COVENANT OF GLASS

On the night of the burial, Marcia tried to leave. She packed her mother's old market basket, planning to slip toward the coast before dawn.

But as she tied the bundle shut, a knock came at her door.

Not a polite knock. Three slow thuds, as though a staff had struck the wood.

Her wrist scar flared, bright as fire under the skin. The basket dropped.

When she opened the door, Elias was there. His single eye caught the lamplight. He did not ask permission to enter. He only tapped the staff once on her floorboards, and her knees folded.

"You made a bargain," he rasped. "You think death cancels debt? Your husband drowned, yes—but your blood still sings. You are mine until I say otherwise."

He led her out. Not with rope, not with chains—just the weight of his will pressing through her scar. Neighbors said later they thought they saw Marcia walking with her head bowed, following a shadow into the cane.

No one stopped her. By morning, her yard was empty. Her absence became another rumor, folded neatly into the village's long history of silences.

~ ~ ~

Marcia was not killed. Elias had no use for corpses. He had uses for vessels.

He kept her in the cane fields at first, hidden in one of the rotting huts the villagers avoided. There were jars stacked in crates—hundreds of small ones. This was his Marketplace. This was where the daily debts lived.

Elias would sit in the half-dark, muttering, and send her to tend them—dusting, turning, listening to the faint noises they made when the moon was high.

"You will keep them company," he told her once. "A woman alone knows the worth of a whisper."

She measured time not by seasons but by Elias's visits. Sometimes he brought her food. Sometimes he brought white rum—ostensibly for the spirits, though he drank most of it himself.

It was on those nights, when the white lightning loosened his tongue, that he spoke of his masterpiece.

He would sit on the dirt floor, the bottle dangling from his hand, and boast of the "Grand Design." He laughed about the young preacher he had turned into a cork to stopper the bottle.

"Thomas thinks he is building a house for God," Elias would cackle, wiping his mouth. "He is building a siphon. Every prayer feeds the glass, Marcia. Every hallelujah makes the dam stronger."

So she knew about the Church. She knew about the Bank beneath the foundation—the heavy anchors he had buried to stop the river.

But she never went there. She was bound to this place, tending the small debts, in the wallet of the Obeah man.

For twenty years, Marcia endured. She grew hollow, her skin tightening over bone. Yet the scar kept her alive.

Then, one night, something changed.

She felt it before Elias did. The scar shivered, not with pain but with release, as though another hand had brushed against the cord that held her. The jars in the hut rattled faintly, unprovoked.

When Elias came the next morning, fury sharpened his voice. "A cork has been touched," he hissed. "The stopper's been disturbed."

He did not look at her when he spoke, but she saw fear twitch in his jaw.

That was when she knew: someone else had entered the story. A child, perhaps. Someone not yet broken by bargains.

The scar loosened enough for her to slip away. Not cleanly—her body still carried the mark—but she found herself on the road, barefoot, staggering into daylight.

To the villagers she looked like ruin, but inside she carried something more dangerous: knowledge.

She walked toward the village of Wataside, her voice raspy with disuse, ready to speak the truth she had carried in the dark.

He never died. But his leash had finally snapped.

CHAPTER 7

The Man Who Studied Silence

Elias was born into the spaces between other people's lives.

He was the son of a cane cutter who had no name outside the payroll ledger, and a mother who scrubbed floors until her fingerprints were worn smooth. He grew up in the dust of the lower valley, a thin, quiet boy with eyes that seemed to swallow light rather than reflect it.

He learned early that the world was a ladder, and his family was the mud at the bottom.

He saw the hierarchy of Clarendon clearly. There were the men who broke their backs in the sun, and there were the men who sat in the shade of the verandas, drinking iced rum. He saw the estate managers drive past in their dusty Land Rovers, wearing crisp white shirts that never seemed to stain.

He saw the shopkeepers who held the power of debt over his father's head.

For a long time, Elias thought money was the only true magic. He ran errands for pennies. He hoarded coins in a tin under the floorboards, believing that if he stacked them high enough, he could climb out of the silence.

But when he was fourteen, the world cracked open and showed him a different kind of ladder.

~ ~ ~

It happened outside the rum shop on a Friday pay-day.

Mr. Pembrook, a wealthy landowner with a voice like gravel and owner of a coffee plantation, was holding court. He was complaining about the laziness of the pickers, his voice booming over the quiet murmur of the men.

In the dust near the steps sat Tata Kojo, as he was known by the locals. Kojo was a rag-man. He lived in a zinc shack by the gully, smelling of woodsmoke and unwashed herbs.

To the church folk, he was a beggar to be pitied. But the older heads knew better. They knew he was an Obeah man— a Shadow Catcher who held court with spirits when the sun went down. Even the stray dogs gave him a wide berth, sensing the heavy, static charge of the grave dirt he carried in his pockets.

Pembrook, turning to leave, stumbled slightly over Kojo's outstretched leg. The landowner didn't apologize. He kicked Kojo's enamel begging bowl, sending the few copper coins scattering into the dirt.

"Move your filth," Pembrook sneered. "You clutter the road."

Elias watched from the shade. He expected Kojo to scramble for the coins. That was the order of things: the boot kicks, and the dog scurries.

But Kojo did not scramble. He stood up slowly. He looked at the wealthy man in the white shirt, and the air around them seemed to go thin and cold.

"You kick my bread today, Mr. Pembrook," Kojo said, his voice low but carrying like a bell. "But the moon sees all debts. Before your coffee is picked, you will kneel in my yard."

Pembrook laughed. He got into his car and drove away, leaving dust in the old man's face. Elias watched him go, thinking the rag-man was a fool to threaten a king.

But the harvest never came for Mr. Pembrook.

First, the blight turned his coffee leaves black. Then, his prize bull fell dead in the pasture, foaming at the mouth. Finally, a fever took his wife—a heat that no doctor in Kingston could cool.

Elias didn't need to witness the night the debt was paid to know it had happened. He saw the evidence in the daylight.

One morning, the fever broke. Pembrook's wife lived. But when Pembrook drove into the village that Sunday, he was a changed man.

He didn't drive with his elbow out the window, waving to the shopkeepers. He gripped the steering wheel with white knuckles, staring straight ahead, avoiding the gaze of the men he used to command.

Then came the whispers that some had seen Mr. Pembrook begging Kojo for mercy. The house staff spoke of the car leaving the estate long after midnight. They spoke of mud on the master's knees. Rumor had it that Pembrook offered money as he begged Kojo to remove whatever spells he had cast.

The village called it gossip. Elias believed.

Kojo had said: You will kneel. And Pembrook had knelt.

In that moment, the coins in Elias's tin box felt like heavy, useless stones.

He realized he had been worshipping the wrong god. Money was powerful, yes. But money was fragile. It could be rotted, burned, or stolen.

But Obeah? Obeah was the wind. You couldn't bankrupt a shadow.

Elias developed a new hunger in his belly. He didn't want to be rich anymore. He wanted to be the man the rich men feared.

~ ~ ~

He did not go to Kojo. He went further.

He used every penny he had to send away for the books the Pastor warned against—thick, heavy parcels wrapped in brown paper that arrived from Chicago.

The Great Book of Magical Art. The writings of L.W. de Laurence.

He read them by the light of a stolen candle while his parents slept. He learned the geometry of spirits. He learned that the world was bound by invisible strings, and if you knew the right knots, you could make the puppets dance.

He practiced in the silence.

He soured a neighbor's milk with a glance. He whispered a name into a jar of vinegar, and a foreman broke his leg the next day. He learned that power was a muscle; it grew when you tore it.

By the time he was twenty, the village of Wataside knew his name. They didn't speak it with love. They spoke it with a drop of their voice, a glance over the shoulder. Elias lived in a hut that smelled of sulfur and ozone, and he drank their fear like wine.

~ ~ ~

His legend was cemented in the drought of '63.

The sky turned to iron. The earth cracked open, gasping. The cane turned yellow in the fields, and the prayers in the church yielded nothing but dust. The heat was democratic; it killed the rich man's crop just as dead as the poor man's garden.

A delegation came to Elias's door. One by one they came. It wasn't just farmers. It was the shopkeeper. It was the deacon. It was the overseers. They all stood in the dirt, sweat staining their shirts.

"Bring the rain, Elias," they begged. "The valley is dying."

Elias looked at them. Men who had once looked through him were now looking at him. They were waiting for his word.

He took their offering. He drew a circle in the dust. For three days, he chanted the words de Laurence had written, twisting the atmosphere like a wet rag.

On the fourth day, the sky broke.

It didn't rain; it poured. A deluge that filled the tanks, greened the hills, and saved the harvest. The entire valley drank because Elias allowed it. No one questioned whether it was luck or magic. They were just relieved, so they believed.

His stature grew as days became weeks, weeks to months. They didn't just fear him anymore. They revered him.

He was the Shepherd of the Storm. He had done what the politicians and the preachers could not. He was the unchecked King of Wataside.

~ ~ ~

The story of the Rainmaker traveled. It crawled out of the valley and reached the ears of men in Kingston who did not believe in magic, but who believed in money and results.

Marcus Sterling arrived in a black car that looked like a hearse. He was a man of business, a representative of the Syndicate—American money, Jamaican land, and endless ambition.

"My clients want the lower valley," Sterling told him, standing in Elias's yard, sweating in his linen suit. "We want to plant cane where the marsh is. But the river is stubborn. The engineers say it cannot be drained."

Sterling looked at the young Obeah man. He saw the poverty, the rags. But he also saw the way the villagers gave Elias a wide berth. He saw the authority.

"They say you command the elements," Sterling said. "Is it a trick?"

Elias looked at the Peace River flowing in the distance. It was heavy, ancient, and indifferent. It was the only thing in the valley that hadn't bowed to him.

"I don't do tricks," Elias said softly.

"Then prove it," Sterling challenged. "We don't need rain. We need a wall. Stop the river, Elias. Dry out the land. Do that, and you won't just be a village witch. You'll be a partner."

Elias felt the thrill of it rise in his throat. He was thrilled at the sound of a partnership; it validated him, gave him status. But that was not what tempted him. It was the audacity. To bind a river was to wrestle a god.

If he won, he would no longer be the boy in the dust. He would be the Architect.

"I will give you the land," Elias said, his eyes fixed on the water. "But the river... the river belongs to me."

He turned his face toward the water and an audacious plan began to form. He did not know then that the river had a memory. He did not know that when you put a chain on a god, you must never, ever let go of the other end.

CHAPTER 8
The Scars We Keep

When Williams stumbled away, the spell broke.

He left behind a silence that was heavier than the shouting had been. His sins had been dragged into the open, his authority cracked like old plaster. The villagers stood in the dust, looking from the retreating white robes to the woman standing in the center of the yard.

Marcia Brown stood alone. She was a stain on the afternoon—ragged, dirty, and smelling of twenty years of confinement.

The crowd did not dissolve all at once. They lingered in uneasy knots along the roadside, whispering low, their glances cutting toward her. Their stares held more fear than pity. To them, she wasn't a victim; she was a carrier. She had brought the "taint" back from the cane fields.

Caro hovered close to Zion. Her hand was clamped on his shoulder, pulling him into her side. Her heart pounded with the helplessness of a mother who had no weapon against spirits.

She looked at Marcia. She saw the ruin of a woman she had known as a girl. But she also saw the only person who knew the name of the enemy.

Caro stepped forward.

"Come," she said. Her voice was steady, though her stomach clenched. "You can't stay in the street."

Marcia turned her head slowly, as if surprised anyone would claim her. A flicker of gratitude passed through her hollow eyes, faint as a coal in the wind.

She followed Caro and Zion down the lane.

~ ~ ~

Caro's house was one of the humbler ones in Wataside— board walls weathered soft and gray, seams chinked with newspaper paste. A zinc roof covered it, patched with tar. It wasn't a fortress, but when Caro bolted the door and dropped the wooden bar, it felt like one.

At the center of the front room sat a table scarred with years of knife marks. This was where life happened, separated from the kitchen by a thin board wall. A wide doorway, always open, linked the two rooms, allowing Caro to look from her work at the coal pot stove directly into the front room and toward the family Bible, which rested on a small ledge inside the hall.

In the kitchen, an open fire pit sat beside the stove, its smoke escaping through a wire-mesh gap between the top of the wooden walls and the zinc roof. The rafters above were polished black with the oily soot of a thousand roasted breadfruits. Here, work counters and narrow shelves for lard and tins were built directly into the back wall of the house, keeping everything she needed within a hand's reach of the heat.

Caro sat stiff-backed at the table. Zion shifted in the corner, one knee pulled to his chest, the black stone a lump in his pocket. Between them, Marcia hunched on a low stool.

THE COVENANT OF GLASS

The lamp hissed as the oil wick caught, throwing a dim, uneasy light across the room.

Without warning, Marcia reached out and turned her wrist upward.

Under the lamplight, the scar gleamed—a pale, puckered cross carved deep into her flesh. It was not fresh, yet it seemed to breathe with its own faint heat.

Caro inhaled sharply. She had seen many wounds in her life, but this one carried intention. It was no accident of cane or blade.

"The price I pay," Marcia rasped. "One drop of blood bind me. Two marks to keep me his. Twenty years, and it still burns when he calls."

She tapped the scar with a brittle finger. Her whole arm trembled.

Caro turned to Zion. The boy looked exhausted, his eyes heavy, the "Prosecutor" gone, leaving a frightened child behind.

"And you," Caro said, turning to the boy, her voice trembling. "That night you come back with your cuffs wet. Tell me what happen."

Zion's eyes darted to the window, to the shadow of the mango tree swaying against the glass.

"I… I don't know," he whispered. "I try to see it, Mama, but it slip away. Like dream-water when you wake. I hear voices, sometimes. I feel heat in my hand. But the river—"

He stopped. His throat worked, but no words came.

Marcia leaned forward. "He can't remember. That's how it binds. Take away the path back so he can't know what he is carrying."

Caro was puzzled by her words.

Zion's fists tightened. Slowly, with a kind of shame, he opened one palm.

Resting there was The Stone. Oval, smooth, dark as midnight. In the dim light it pulsed faintly, a low, rhythmic throb.

Caro's chair screeched as she shot to her feet.

"God above," she gasped, pressing a hand to her chest. She snatched forward, ready to grab it. "Throw it 'way! Out the door, into the bush!"

Zion jerked back, curling his fingers tight. "No, Mama!" His voice cracked, but his grip was iron.

Marcia's voice cut through the air. "Don't."

Caro spun on her. "Don't? You see the thing? It's burning him! It is not natural!"

Marcia held up her scar again.

"Natural never saved me, Caro. But that stone… that stone is the only reason he is still sitting here."

Caro froze. "What you mean?"

"Look at him," Marcia said. "Elias is trying to enter him. He is using the boy as a door. Usually, a vessel breaks under that pressure. The mind snaps. The soul gets pushed out."

She pointed at the black rock in Zion's fist.

"But he has a Counter-weight," Marcia said softly. "It burns him, yes. But it anchors him. It is heavy enough to keep his own soul in his body. If you throw that stone away, Zion floats away with it. And Elias takes the empty house."

Caro slowly lowered her hand. She looked at her son— thin, terrified, clutching a piece of the riverbed as if it were a life raft.

"You sure?" she asked, her voice brittle.

"I don't know its true purpose," Marcia admitted. "But I know Elias didn't give it. Elias fears it. It is something set against him."

The lamp sputtered. Outside, the wind pushed a branch against the window with a hollow scrape.

"Tell me," Caro said, sitting back down. "You live twenty years under him. Tell me how he works."

Marcia's lips twisted into a bitter smile.

"He deals in Want," she said. "A woman wants her husband. A pastor wants a crowd. You give him your want, and he binds it to something dear. A token. A scrap of bone. That way, your debt has a house."

"The Glass Jars," Caro said.

Marcia nodded. "His storehouse. Every bargain sealed, every secret held—it's bottled and waiting. I tended the small ones. The daily debts. The love spells and the petty curses."

She hesitated, her eyes darkening.

"But there are others. Bigger ones. I never saw them, but I felt them. The Heavy Anchors. The ones marked with Blue Wax."

Caro frowned. "Blue wax?"

"Blue wax," Marcia whispered. "Blood debts. Lives traded for power. Those are the ones that hold the big magic. If those break… the whole valley shakes."

Caro's fingers dug into the table. She thought of Samuel, Zion's father. She thought of the silence that had swallowed him, and the rumors that had always pointed to Elias.

"And if we break them?" Caro asked, her voice tight. "If we break the jars, is Zion free?"

Marcia shook her head. "Destroying them weakens Elias, yes. It starves him. But it don't unmake the bargain. Sometimes what's loosed is worse than what's kept."

Zion stirred on his mat. He had fallen asleep sitting up, his head tipping against the wall, his hand still curved protectively around The Stone.

Caro watched him. Then she looked at the ruined woman across the table.

"I don't care about the valley," Caro said, her voice hard and low. "I care about him. You said knowledge don't save."

"It doesn't," Marcia agreed.

"Then we make it a weapon," Caro said. "You know where the bodies are buried, Marcia. You know where the cracks are."

She reached across the table and covered Marcia's scarred hand with her own.

Then Caro stood up. She went to the darker corner of the room, behind the chest, where dust motes danced in the low light. She returned a moment later holding a walking stick—a sturdy piece of lignum vitae, polished smooth by the grip of the woman who had lived in this house before her.

She pressed the heavy wood into Marcia's trembling hand.

"You teach me how to guard him," Caro said. "And I will help you break the glass. Here. Take this. You will need it."

Marcia's fingers closed around the handle. It was the first thing she had owned in twenty years. She tested the weight of it, finding a balance she thought she had lost.

"We start tomorrow," Marcia whispered. "Because the Pastor is afraid. And a frightened man digs deep holes."

She looked up at Caro, her gaze sharpening.

"But you must learn the rules, Caro," Marcia said. "If we are to hunt him, we use the things he hates. Salt. Moving water. And above all... silence."

The lamp hissed. The night pressed closer.

Two women sat with their fear between them—one marked by a scar, the other by a mother's desperation—and in that dim kitchen, the resistance began.

CHAPTER 9
The Dividing Line

The house was quiet, but Caro could not sleep.

She lay staring at the rafters, listening to the steady rise and fall of Zion's breath beside her and the dry, rattling exhale of Marcia on the cot.

Every time she closed her eyes, her mind pulled her back to old places. Not dreams exactly, but memories that came crowding when the dark was long.

She had been no older than Zion when Marcia Brown vanished from the village—nine, maybe ten. Though she hadn't understood the full weight of it then, she remembered the change that followed: doors shut earlier, women spoke in lowered voices at the standpipe, men turned their faces away at the crossroads. Nobody said Elias, but the name was written on every silence.

That was the first time she learned how fear could settle over a community like a heavy cloth.

Her thoughts wandered further, to the open wound of her own youth.

She had been a bright student, always reading, quick to answer. Her teachers said she would go far if chance allowed. Her family had little, but they held her to high standards, and she tried to carry their hopes.

At seventeen, she fell in love with Samuel.

He was a boy she had known since primary school. He had even less than she did, but he possessed a brilliant mind —sharper than hers, she often thought. They shared big dreams. They both earned the grades to enter high school. But Samuel dropped out two years later when his father died of cancer, leaving the family broken and poor.

He gave up school to help his mother. For a while, he worked at the shop for less than he deserved, paid partly in groceries, but it kept them going.

They talked of marriage. When she became pregnant at eighteen, he shouldered the burden with a fierce resolve. Wanting more for her, for the child, he took extra work running errands for Elias.

"It's harmless, Caro," he had told her, his eyes bright with the promise of coin. "Only carrying letters and parcels. Nothing of obeah or bargains."

She believed him because she wanted to.

But one day he went on a run toward Morgan's Pass and never returned.

The stories swirled—some said thieves took him. Some said he ran away. Most whispered one name—Elias. No body was ever found. No burial, no grave. Just silence, and Caro standing at her door each evening, waiting for footsteps that never returned.

That was when silence became her armor. At the standpipe, when women hinted. In church, when Pastor Williams thundered about sin but never named the Obeah man. In her own yard, when she swore she would raise her son without drawing Elias's eye.

Silence, she thought, might keep them safe.

Now the silence was breaking. The morning Zion first spoke strange words that were not his own, a foreboding had seized her, sharp and cold, as if Samuel's ghost had brushed past. With Marcia's return and her talk of bondage, Caro felt the grip of the past tighten. But alongside it, something new took root.

She would not lose her son to the same silence. If it cost her everything, she would fight.

~ ~ ~

By dawn, the lane outside was alive.

The standpipe ran early. Pans clanged against enamel basins; the sound of hooves marked the passing of herds along the track.

Word had spread faster than the sun. The village knew about Marcia walking barefoot through the heat haze. They knew about Zion speaking hidden sins. They knew about Pastor Williams dropping his Bible in the dust.

When Caro stepped into the yard with her basin, the voices stopped.

Patch crept from under the steps, tail low. He followed her to the gate, then sat, watching the lane as though it had grown unfamiliar overnight.

At the standpipe, Sister Etta stood with her jaw tight, knuckles white on the handle of her bucket. Auntie Myra was beside her, her face worn from tears. Others came and went, moving slower than usual, eyes sliding sideways.

"Morning," Caro said, setting her basin down.

The greeting hung in the air, heavy and unanswered.

"The pastor hand not clean," a woman muttered finally, staring into her bucket.

Another answered quickly, "Then whose clean? If him fall, what left to hold?"

"He not holding much," a third woman whispered. "You never see the rectory window? Light burn straight through the night. Shadow passing back and forth like a caged tiger. The man not sleeping. He wrestling with something."

From the shade of the almond tree, a thin man—one of the cane cutters—spat into the dust.

"So what the boy be then?" he asked, his voice carrying. "Prophet, or devil mouth?"

The water splash stopped. Children stilled their play.

Caro straightened. She felt the heat rising in her neck, but her voice was calm, her diction precise.

"He is my son," she said. "Not prophet. Not devil. A child who spoke what grown folk already knew but were too coward to say."

Heads turned toward her, sharp and defensive.

"Known?" the man scoffed. "A child can't know them things. Somebody teaching him."

Caro met his gaze. "Somebody been teaching Elias long before my boy was born."

Silence thickened. It was a dangerous silence. Buckets overflowed into basins, the water spilling across bare feet.

One woman near the pipe turned on her. "So is our fault now? You want to put the curse on us?"

Caro held steady. "I kept quiet when Samuel never came home from Morgan's Pass. My silence fed Elias same as any offering. We all kept quiet. That's how he grew."

Uneasy murmurs spread. No one wanted to agree, but the truth of it was a hook in their mouths.

Then the man by the tree sneered. "And the witch? You bring the jailer into your house. She bring trouble back with her."

"She came back with a warning," Caro said. "Elias is weak. You saw him yesterday—the Pastor ran. The Obeah man is not as strong as he wants you to believe. Fear feeds him. Keep feeding, and you build the road he needs."

"He feeds on your doubt."

The rasping voice cut through the morning chatter like a saw.

Marcia Brown had stepped out of Caro's gate. She stood in the road, thin and hollow-eyed, looking like a scarecrow that had walked off its post.

The crowd recoiled.

"You think fear protects you?" Marcia said. She didn't shout, but her voice carried the weight of the grave. "It fattens him. Every whisper, every sideways look, every curse on the boy's head—it is meat for Elias."

She walked toward the standpipe. The circle opened wide to let her pass.

"He cannot rise on strength alone," Marcia said. "He needs the road you build with your fear. Don't lay the stones for him."

The man by the almond tree shifted his weight, looking uneasy. "So what we do, then? Fight a duppy with a stick?"

Marcia looked at him. Her eyes were empty holes.

"Weakness is what he sells," she said. "Fear is the price. Resolve is the only thing he cannot eat. You want to fight? Then stop feeding him."

No one moved. But the line was drawn. Some eyes stayed hard—doubtful, cold, ready to blame. Others, like Etta's, softened—terror replaced by a desperate need for direction.

From the edge of the crowd, a voice rose—low but clear.

"So how we do that, Marcia?"

Marcia looked at the Peace River flowing silently in the distance.

"We stop hiding," she said. "And we watch the water."

CHAPTER 10
The First Jar

To understand the fire that was coming, one had to
understand the spark.

Marcia Brown did not know a boy was standing by the
river. She did not know a stone was pulsing in a pocket. For
twenty years, her world had been the size of a hut—a twelve-
by-twelve box of rotting cedar and corrugated zinc, hidden
deep in the unharvested rows where the cane grew thick and
the sun rarely touched the ground.

She measured time not by clocks, but by the jars.

They were stacked against the walls in crates, hundreds
of them. This was the Marketplace. The "Bank"—the heavy
foundation jars—was hidden under the church, but these
were the daily accounts. The petty jealousies, the love spells,

the small sicknesses traded for coin. They hummed in the dark, a choir of trapped whispers.

For twenty years, she had endured—hollowing, her skin tightening over bone, her voice fading to a rasp. Yet the scar on her wrist kept her alive, bound to his bargains.

Then, the rhythm changed.

It wasn't a sound. It was a sensation in the bone.

Somewhere in the valley, a seal broke.

It felt like a wire snapping inside her arm.

The welt on her wrist, twenty years old, cooled like quenched iron. Her breath came hard and sudden, a gasp she had not owned in decades.

In the crates against the wall, the jars rattled faintly, unprovoked.

Marcia dropped the dried herbs she was sorting. She stared at her arm. The scar, usually angry and red-rimmed, had gone terrifyingly pale. It shivered, not with pain but with release, as though another hand had brushed against the cord that held her.

She stood up. Her legs were weak, but her heart was hammering.

He failed, she thought. The Jailer dropped a key.

The door banged open.

Elias stood there.

He didn't wait until morning. He had felt the break too.

He looked huge in the doorway, blocking the night. His single eye glittered like wet stone. He wasn't carrying his staff; he was gripping the doorframe so hard the wood splintered. Shadows bent toward him, writhing with his fury.

"A cork has been touched," he hissed. "The stopper's been disturbed."

He stepped into the hut. The rage filled the small space, sucking the air out of the room. Yet Marcia saw what he tried to mask: a twitch at his jaw, the unmistakable flicker of fear.

That was when she knew: someone else had entered the story. An innocent hand, perhaps. Someone not yet broken by bargains.

"You," he snarled, looking at her slack scar. "You think a broken seal frees you?"

He lunged.

He didn't move like an old man. He moved like a shadow lengthening at sunset—fast and fluid.

"Your blood is my seal," he roared. "One cut, and the cord holds again."

He grabbed for her wrist, his fingernails sharpened like claws, intending to reopen the wound and rebind the spell with fresh blood.

But the scar refused him. His hand slipped off her skin as if she were oiled. The magic had no purchase. The circuit was broken.

Marcia didn't think. Instinct, buried under twenty years of obedience, flared hot. She swung the kerosene lamp at him.

It smashed against his chest. It didn't burn him—he was too cold for that—but the glass shattered, and the oil splashed him. He recoiled, hissing.

Marcia turned and bolted for the cane.

She burst out of the hut into the night.

The air was thick and humid. The cane stalks towered over her, ten to twelve feet high, a wall of rattling green blades.

"Marcia!"

The scream came from behind her. It was a command. Usually, that voice would buckle her knees. Usually, the scar would burn so hot she would curl into a ball.

But tonight, her wrist was cool.

She ran barefoot through the dirt. She stumbled, weakened by twenty years of drained strength, but she twisted upright and staggered deeper into the rows.

Behind her, the cane crashed. Elias was giving chase. He was tearing through the field, roaring. He was gaining.

She saw the break in the cane ahead—the edge of the compound where the cleared land met the wild bush.

He will catch me, she thought. He is stronger.

She reached the edge and fell onto the grass, scrambling around, crab-walking backward, waiting for the blow.

Elias burst through the cane row. He raised his hand, ready to drag her back.

He took one step out of the cane.

BOOM.

The earth in front of him flared.

THE COVENANT OF GLASS

A line of fire—thin, blue, and impossibly hot—scorched across the soil at his feet. It wasn't natural fire; it was the color of burning gas.

Elias slammed into an invisible wall.

He was thrown backward, landing hard in the dirt. He scrambled up, shrieking with rage, and threw himself at the boundary again. He swerved left, seeking a gap, but the glow followed, circling him, searing the ground wherever he pressed.

Hiss.

The air shimmered. He couldn't cross.

Marcia stared, panting. She looked at the line of blue fire, then at the man pacing behind it like a caged tiger.

She understood.

"The Jars," she whispered, her voice rasping from disuse.

Elias gripped the invisible bars of his prison. His face was contorted in fury and disbelief.

"You bound the river to the land," Marcia said. "But you bound yourself too, Elias. You tied your life to the Anchor. You can't leave the radius of the Vault."

Elias struck the barrier, sparks flying.

"You have nowhere to go!" he screamed, his voice cracking. "The world out there has forgotten you! You will die in the dark!"

"Maybe," Marcia said, standing up. Her legs were shaking, but they held her weight. "But I won't die in here."

She turned her back on him.

She walked into the dark. Behind her, his roar tore after her, the sound of power straining at its tether—a leash pulled taut, snapping but not breaking. She walked for an hour or two until she saw the distant lights of Wataside.

PART 2
The Watchman Cannot Leave the Gate

Chapter 11

The Pastor's Dream

Many decades before, the book had come from New Orleans, hidden in a crate of salted cod fish to pass the customs agents at the Kingston wharf. It was heavy, bound in black fabric that smelled of mildew and burnt sage. On the spine, in fading gold leaf, was the name: L.W. de Laurence.

Elias sat in the small room behind the shop—long before he built the church—and turned the pages with a trembling finger.

He wasn't looking for love spells or curses. He was looking for dominion.

He found it on page 214: The Rite of the Still Water.

The diagram showed a river depicted as a serpent. A spike was driven through the serpent's heart, pinning it to the earth.

"To quiet the Fluid Spirit," the text read, "one must first remove the Pulse. The Heart of the river must be severed and hidden in silence."

Elias smiled. He traced the drawing of the spike. It was exactly what the Syndicate needed. They wanted dry land for cane; he would give them a desert.

But his finger stopped at the footnote. It was written in smaller, red type—a warning from the author.

"WARNING: A dam made of glass cannot hold a river of spirit. The pressure will shatter it. To hold the water against its will, the Sorcerer must become the Mortar. He must bind his own life to the foundation to keep the seal tight. But take heed:

To bind the river to the spot is to bind the binder to the spot. The Watchman cannot leave the Gate."

Elias stared at the words.

The Watchman cannot leave.

He looked out the window at the lush, green valley of Wataside...

He dipped his pen in the inkwell.

With a steady hand, he drew a thick black line through the warning, crossing it out.

"I am not the Watchman," Elias whispered to the empty room. "I am the King."

He closed the book. The deal was made.

~ ~ ~

The river knew before the village did.

Down where the current ran black and cold, Elias felt the loss as pain. It was not a mystery to him which jar had failed. He knew the weight of each debt the way a fisherman knows the heft of each net. Marcia's tether had gone slack. The thread that kept her mind within his reach had snapped, and in its place the water pressed hard, narrowing the space he could claim as his own.

He tested his edges and found them closer than yesterday. Where he had once stretched along the bend and into the side cane-ditch, he now met resistance. The river did not open when he pushed; it pushed back.

Hunger rose in him like a fever. For twenty years he had managed the river's appetite by turning it into contracts— wants made into tokens, tokens sealed into jars that fed him slow and steady. Control had been the point. Control, and safety. Spirits were an unruly breed; they did what they were sent to do, and then they did what they wanted. In his youth he had used them freely and paid for it with scars no one could see. In age, he had avoided them, preferring jars and silence.

But Marcia was gone from his hand. His cage had tightened. Safety was a word for men with time, and his time was thinning. Elias needed to know how much of his reach remained. With the jars failing and the foundation bleeding, he had to see if the village still belonged to his will, or if he was truly fading into the cold silt.

He drew in the river's cold through every part of himself —raw, unrefined energy to replace the "stored" power of the broken jars—and let it loose in a single sound. The cry boiled the surface for a breath and sent fish knifing for deeper shadow. It wasn't a cry of pain; it was a sonar strike, a vibration sent traveling through the mud and up into the foundations of the lane.

No human ear would have called it a voice, but the dogs up in the lane lifted their heads and whined, feeling the shiver in the dirt. A child sleeping near the standpipe turned over and pulled the sheet to her chin, her small spike of terror traveling back down the thread to Elias like a bell ringing in the dark.

Elias stilled. The echo was faint—too faint. He was thinning. He could waste himself roaring. Or he could begin again the way he had begun before the jars—by sending. Not a body. Not a storm. Not yet. Whispers first. Small fires. A face at a door. Enough to stir the village's fear and make strength run back into him like blood into a withered limb.

It was risk. Spirits remembered old debts and found their own paths. They could nip at the hand that loosed them. But the choice was no longer between safe and dangerous. It was between fading and holding on.

He reached for what he still held: the lattice of jars along the riverbed, each a knot in the rope that pinned the Lady to her course. In their glass lay scraps of hair and blood and love, scraps of shame and rage and need—fuel, but also channels. Through those channels he drew a thread of power and divided it, thin as smoke. He sent one thread climbing the bank to the lane where the little houses sat close. He sent another into the mind of the man who had once begged on his dirt and risen on his name.

As the threads left his fingers, the gray mud of the riverbank seemed to creep higher up his legs, claiming more of his essence in exchange for the reach.

Then he waited, pressing himself against the cold to keep what strength remained from leaking away.

~ ~ ~

Pastor Williams did not remember lying down. He woke in his clothes most nights now, the white shirt wrinkled under his back, his throat sore from prayers that had not changed the shape of his shame. The image of himself in the yard—Bible on the dust, eyes of his congregation turned to stone—had not faded. It followed him from room to room and lay under his pillow like a rock.

Sleep took him hard and without mercy. The dream did not ask his leave.

It began in the cane fields on a Tuesday so hot the air wobbled. Elias sat on a low stool, his staff across his knees, one eye bright and the other hidden under cloth gone brown with sweat. Williams saw himself as he had been then: a young man with clean shoes and a voice too big for his shed-sized church, kneeling because standing felt like lying.

"You lack patience," Elias had said, and the way he had said the word made it taste like a sin. He reached out and pressed the knotted head of his staff—dry, gnarled wood wrapped in blackened leather—into the center of Williams's palm. The touch was brief and cold, and the cold spread like ink through paper.

"The Lord rewards your ambition," Elias whispered, smiling with his one eye. "Go now. Speak of me no more. Your congregation will grow, but your debt is eternal."

The dream turned. The cane was gone. Williams sat at his table in the side room of the church, a quill in his hand and a letter half written. Sir, I cannot—The ink blurred as his hand shook. Release me from the words we spoke—He folded the paper with fingers that would not obey him, pressed the crease with the heel of his palm, and could not make himself carry it to the hut. He slid the letter behind a Bible and laid his silence on top of it like a lid.

The dream turned again. The ground behind the church was brown and hard, the sun struck bright, and the congregation stood thick and hopeful while he took the first spade of earth from the spot where the sanctuary would rise. Hymns lifted behind him, voices made bigger by the open air. His chest had filled then. He had told himself it was the Holy Spirit. He had told himself many things.

The ground shifted under his feet. The hymn thinned and widened into a roar. The churchyard flowed outward, seats rising in steep ranks, towers rearing against the sky. Floodlights burned down like second suns. He stood at the center of Kingston's National Stadium, and the stands were full beyond counting. Hands rose in the tens of thousands, a forest of arms, and his name rolled through the concrete bowl in waves: Pastor. Pastor. Pastor.

He opened his Bible. The pages were blank. It did not matter. His mouth shaped words and the sound of them surged up the steel girders and out along invisible paths to radios and televisions and the little boxes in kitchens where families ate. He felt the weight of the island turn toward him.

He lifted his eyes to the highest row. A single eye blinked in the dark. Not in a face. Just the eye. It was patient as a tide.

The roar of the crowd didn't fade, but it grew muffled, dull, as if hearing a choir through a thick window. The air in the dream suddenly chilled, smelling not of sulfur or ambition, but of deep, churning mud and wet stone.

He looked down at the front rows. The people were screaming his name, their mouths wide... they were pressing their hands against invisible walls. They were not just sitting; they were contained. Thousands of them, curled and cramping, packed into spaces too small, waiting for a hand to shatter the barrier.

The glass hummed. It was the same hum he had heard coming from the jars in Elias's hut all those years ago.

A voice ran under the muffled roar, close as breath. They are waiting, Thomas. They are not lost. They are kept. Break the glass, and the harvest is yours.

He woke with his hand clawing at the bedclothes... Sweat ran from his temples into his collar. The room was dark, the window a dull square. He pressed his palms together and bowed his head because prayer had always looked like that in picture books, but the words that rose in him were not confession. They were a kind of hunger.

He sat there until the window went from dull to gray. In that small light, he saw his white shirt rumpled and did not fix it. He saw his Bible on the table and picked it up, not to read but to feel its weight. Before the sun cleared the trees he stepped into the yard, eyes red with the night, back straight the way a back learns to be straight when people are looking.

Forgiveness was still a long way off, but fear has a way of making old enemies look like saviors. They didn't trust the shepherd anymore, but they were too terrified of the dark to leave the fold.

He did not smile. He did not need to. The dream burned behind his eyes like a lantern and lit the road.

~ ~ ~

The child woke before it was light outside.

Her mother felt the sudden stiffness of her body on the mat and was up in a breath, hand on the little shoulder. "What is it? What you hear?"

The girl pointed at the door. Her finger shook. "He call me."

"Who call you?"

"Uncle."

The mother's mouth tightened. The girl's uncle had been buried three years ago under a tamarind tree with a good hymn and a decent crowd. "You see him?"

"No." The girl's eyes did not leave the door. "Him outside. Him say my name. Two times."

Her mother's hand slid to the back of the girl's head and pressed there, gentle but firm. "When a voice you can't see call your name, you answer once and then keep your mouth shut," she said because her own grandmother had said it to her and because the words knew the path out of her mouth without thinking. "You hear me?"

The girl nodded into her mother's chest. Her heart beat like a bird's.

They did not open the door. The mother sat with the child's head in her lap until the birds came into the mango tree and the gray of the window turned to thin yellow. Only then did she go outside. She did not expect to see anything.

She saw the print of a heel turned sideways in the dust, as if someone had stood there uncertain. It could have been a child's. It could have been nothing.

By the time she reached the standpipe, the story had already stretched. She said it plain to Sister Etta—"She say Uncle call her twice at the door"—and Etta's mouth set into a thin line. "A child must keep quiet after the first call," Etta said, and then, because fear likes company, she told Auntie Myra, and by midday people were saying a voice had called at three doors, and by afternoon someone swore the voice had knocked, and by evening duppy had become the word people used because it was better to use a word you knew than to say a thing you feared without a name.

No one said Elias. They did not need to. The name moved in their minds the way a shark moves under dark water—felt, not seen.

Patch paced the lane until the sun was properly up, paws scoring the dust, head low, nose working. He would not pass the gate of the child's yard. When the girl came outside to look at the print by the door, he stood crosswise to her and wagged once, uncertain, and then went to lie under Caro's step with his body pressed long and tight as a board, ears up, waiting.

Caro watched from her doorway as the village woke with a shiver. The normal rhythm of Wataside was gone, replaced by a jittery, fearful energy that made every opening door sound like a warning.

She heard the new softness in the way people spoke to Pastor Williams as he passed, and she felt the old fear try to get its hand around her throat. She set her palm on the doorframe to keep it steady. In the back room, Zion turned in his sleep and drew his hand over the shape in his pocket as if to check it was still there.

In the river, Elias held himself still and counted his strength in slow measures. The sending had found its mark. The village had flinched. His hunger eased by a finger's width. It would not be enough for long. Risk had paid him once. He would pay it again.

He pressed his face toward the surface, not to breathe— he had not done that in years—but to listen. Voices carried differently over water. He listened for the sound he needed most: the thin, high thread that ran through a crowd when fear gathered. When he heard it, he would send again.

CHAPTER 12
The Hunt Begins

The sun that morning was not kind. It rose white and hard, bleaching the color from the hills and pressing down on the zinc roofs until the heat shimmered off the metal dancing vapors.

Pastor Williams did not wait for Sunday. By eight o'clock, the church bell was ringing—not the steady toll for service, but a rapid, clanging alarm that pulled women from their wash tubs and men from their domino tables.

They gathered in the dust of the churchyard, squinting against the glare. The Pastor stood on the concrete steps. He had not shaved. His white shirt was open at the collar, damp with sweat, but his eyes were clear, terrifyingly bright. He looked like a man who had stared into the sun and liked what he saw.

"We have been sleeping!" he shouted, his voice cracking the heavy air. He did not hold a Bible. He held a shovel, its blade rusted and caked with old earth.

The crowd rippled, uneasy. Sister Etta adjusted her headwrap, glancing at Auntie Myra. They were used to a shepherd who spoke of patience and tithes. They did not know this man who gripped a garden tool like a weapon.

"For twenty years," Williams roared, pacing the narrow step, "we lived in shadow. We whispered about the cane fields. We walked wide of the river. We thought we were hiding from the devil." He stopped, pointing the shovel at them. "But the devil is a liar, and we believed him!"

He stepped down into the dust, moving among them. "Why did Marcia Brown come back? Tell me! Was it because we prayed? Was it because she was strong?"

Silence answered him.

"She came back," Williams hissed, lowering his voice so they had to lean in, "because a jar broke."

A murmur went through the crowd. He had said the forbidden thing.

"We thought the jars were prisons for demons," Williams cried, raising his voice again, swinging his arms wide as if addressing the stadium of his dream. He didn't tell them that Marcia had whispered for him to gather the jars with the care one might use for a sleeping viper. Ever since the failed exorcism, that word had rotted in his mind. Gathering meant keeping—it meant the secrets still existed. He didn't want to keep them; he wanted them gone.

"But the Lord showed me the truth last night!" he continued, the lie smooth and practiced. "They are not prisons for evil. They are storehouses for us! They are holding our blessings! They are suppressing our prosperity. They are holding the souls of this village, cramping them in glass, waiting for a faithful hand to set them free!"

He looked at Myra. "Your peace, sister? It is in a bottle in the earth." He looked at the men. "Your strength? It is corked and waxed, waiting for you."

He raised the shovel high. "The Lord said to me: Break the glass, Thomas, and the harvest is yours. Who is ready to harvest?"

101

It was a lie born of a dream, but to a village steeped in fear and shame, it tasted like salvation. It offered them a way to fight back.

"I ready, Pastor!" a young man shouted. "Me too," another called. "Mash them down!" Etta cried, her fear turning sharp and aggressive.

They moved like a single beast. They did not go to the fields to cut cane; they went to turn the earth, seeking the promised harvest sealed within the glass. Men brought pickaxes and machetes. Women brought garden forks and hoe-sticks. Children ran behind, caught up in the fever, carrying stones.

Caro stood at her gate, watching the procession stream past. She gripped Zion's shoulder so hard her knuckles turned pale.

"They don't know," she whispered. "Lord have mercy, they don't know what they're digging for."

Zion watched Pastor Williams leading the march, his white shirt flapping. The boy's hand went to his pocket. The Stone was cold, but when the Pastor passed, it gave a single, hard throb against his thigh.

THE COVENANT OF GLASS

~ ~ ~

The cane field was a wall of green and gold, rattling in the windless heat. The villagers spread out, hacking at the roots, overturning the soil. It was chaotic, desperate work.

"Here! The dog find one!"

The shout came from near the irrigation ditch. Patch was there. The dog was frantic, digging at the mud with erratic, terrified strokes, whining high in his throat. He would dig, then back away snarling, then dig again, his instincts warring with his terror. He smelled the unnatural scent of the River leaking up through the soil, and he was trying to expose the threat.

But the villagers saw only a pointer.

"Good boy!" a man cheered, shoving the dog aside. "He smell the devil work!"

The man struck the earth with his pickaxe. Once. Twice.

Clink.

The sound was dull, glass against metal. The crowd surged forward, circling tight. The man fell to his knees and scraped away the dirt.

There were three of them. Mason jars, old and clouded, the wax seals black with age. They sat nestled in the roots like dark eggs.

"Break them!" Williams commanded from the edge of the circle. "Release the captives!"

The man raised his pickaxe.

"In the name of the Father!" he shouted, and brought the metal down.

Kr-crash.

The first jar shattered. Then the second. Then the third.

The villagers flinched, bracing for a scream, a shadow, a demon.

But there was no scream. There was only a sound like a soft sigh—hiss—as the vacuum inside the jars equalized with the outside air.

Then, the change.

It didn't happen in the sky. It happened in the ground. The soil where the jars had broken suddenly turned dark. Water seeped up around the man's boots—not clear water, but thick, brown slurry, smelling of rotted leaves and stagnant pools.

The air in the cane field instantly grew heavier. The dry heat vanished, replaced by a suffocating, wet blanket of humidity that made sweat cling to skin like syrup.

"You feel that?" Williams whispered, his eyes wide and ecstatic. He spread his hands, mistaking the crushing pressure of the rising river for the weight of glory. "The Spirit is descending! The power is loose!"

"Hallelujah!" Etta screamed, falling to her knees in the mud.

"Find more!" Williams yelled, pointing his shovel at the endless rows of cane. "Dig them all up! Don't leave a single blessing in the ground!"

Far back at the gate, Zion watched the heat haze distort the figures in the field. He saw them cheering. He saw them digging.

But he felt the air change. He felt the moisture settle in his lungs, heavy and tasting of silt. Beside him, Caro shivered despite the heat.

"The air getting wet," Zion whispered, the words falling out of him with a knowledge he hadn't learned. "They puncturing the boat, Mama. And they think the water coming in is a blessing."

~ ~ ~

Elias sensed a change. His plan was askew. The low, rhythmic hum that had been his anchor for twenty years suddenly turned to a discordant shriek in the water.

Elias was slammed against the cold silt of the riverbed. He didn't see the break, but he felt it—a brutal, snapping sensation, like someone ripping nerves out of his spine. The jars were not just releasing water; they were releasing the energy—the pressure he had relied on to hold the water back. Three jars were gone, and the shock of that loss was a physical, dizzying pain that sent him scrambling backward along the mud.

The fools, he thought, rage thickening the current around him. They think it's a harvest.

He had meant for them to be weakened by the whispers, not galvanized into action. He felt the current thicken and turn frigid, the cold pressure of the awakened water squeezing the air from the space he occupied. He was left weak and shaking, listening to the muffled, maniacal cheer of his congregation celebrating his death.

He realized the speed of the catastrophe. If they kept breaking the seals, he wouldn't just be starved; he would be annihilated by the resulting flood. He needed his assets, and he needed them now. He reached out blindly with the last thread of his will—not for the Pastor, who was lost to madness—but for the only asset who still possessed a shred of sense.

He sent the thread climbing the bank to the single place he knew the women still met, pressing a vivid, tempting picture into the mind of his greatest threat.

Go to Prospect, he sent. Come to the far bank.

CHAPTER 13
The First Set of Rules

Night did not bring relief. Usually, the cane fields went quiet after dark, but tonight the air was bruised with sound. Torches flickered in the distance, and the rhythmic thud-thud of metal on earth echoed across the valley. The crusade had not stopped at sundown.

Inside Caro's house, the mood was not victorious. The air felt heavy, damp, and smelling of river silt, though the nearest water was almost a mile away.

Caro sat on the edge of the cot where Zion sat, his knees pulled to his chest. Marcia perched on the stool, her hands folded in her lap. The scar on her wrist was pale, but it was no longer slack—it was twitching, reacting to the violence being done to the earth outside.

"They think they winning," Marcia said, her voice low. "They break three jars today. Maybe four. They say the heavy air is the Spirit descending."

"Is it?" Zion asked. He looked small, The Stone clutched in his hand.

"No," Marcia said. "It is the dam leaking. Elias built those jars to hold debts, yes. But he also built them to hold back the River. He made himself the gatekeeper. If you break the gate without paying the toll, the water don't care who it drowns."

Caro rubbed her arms. The house felt cold despite the humidity. "The Pastor says it's a harvest. He says we are claiming back our blessings."

"The Pastor hungry," Marcia countered. "And a hungry man will eat poison if you serve it on a silver plate. Elias know this. He is feeding the Pastor's pride so the Pastor will break the prison for him, but I don't think it working the way Elias wants. They breaking down his power."

Patch lay at the doorway, nose pressed to the crack beneath the wood. He was not sleeping. Every few minutes he would let out a sharp, high whine, vibrating with a tension that ran through the floorboards.

"We cannot stop them," Caro said, the frustration bitter in her throat. "Not tonight. The fever is on them."

"Then we must protect ourselves," Marcia said. She turned her eyes to Zion. "Because when the water rise up, it look for the lowest point. And when Elias get desperate, him look for the one who started the unraveling."

Zion shrank back against the wall. "Me?"

"You," Marcia said. "It was your hand that broke the first seal. It was your hand that free me. Elias knows."

Caro reached out and covered Zion's hand with hers. "Tell us what to do."

Marcia leaned forward. The lamplight caught the hollows of her face, making her look like a prophetess of old.

"There are rules," she said. "Elias bound himself with laws. To fight him, you must keep them. Listen good, boy."

"First," Marcia said, holding up one finger. "If a voice call you and you can't see the mouth, answer once and no more."

"Why?" Zion whispered. He had asked his mother the same question, but he wanted Marcia's confirmation.

"Because spirits feed on acknowledgment," she replied. "The first answer lets them know you hear. That is only manners. But every word after that is an open door. Each repetition is consent. Permission to draw closer. You hear your name in the dark again, you clamp your teeth shut. You hear?"

Zion nodded, eyes wide.

"Second," she continued. "If a jar come in your hand—and it will, for the earth is vomiting them up now—don't break it in your own yard."

Caro frowned. "The villagers... they bringing them home. I saw Mr. Dawes carrying one in his shirt like a baby."

Marcia closed her eyes briefly, as if in pain. "Then Mr. Dawes is a fool. Jars don't just contain power; they contain what was bargained. Grief. Anger. Hunger. Breaking it releases that force raw. If you do it in your yard, you tie that energy to your house and your bloodline. Your house is no longer your home, it will turn on you."

She looked sharply at Zion. "The only safe place is moving water. The current scatters the debt. If you find one, you take it to the river. Nowhere else."

"Third," she said, pointing to his hand. "Keep The Stone where the river can see it."

Zion opened his fist. The black stone sat there, dull and heavy.

"It isn't Elias's," Marcia said softly. "It is older. It belongs to the thing Elias tried to master. If you hide it away—in a box, in a drawer—it goes blind. It becomes unstable. But carried openly, near your skin, it balances the weight."

Finally, she reached into the small pocket at her waist. She drew out a pinch of white crystals and let them fall onto the table.

"And always carry salt."

Caro looked at the grains. "Salt?"

"The oldest ward," Marcia said. "Spirits recoil from it because it represents preservation. Life. Purity. It burns them like acid burns skin."

She looked at Caro. "It is not a wall. It is a shield. A pinch in the pocket, sprinkled on a threshold, or cast in a circle. It buys you time. A breath or two. Sometimes a breath is all you need to run."

Caro nodded silently. She stood up, went to the kitchen shelf, and took down the tin. She tore three strips of cloth from an old skirt. Into each, she poured a measure of salt, tying them into tight, hard knots.

She pressed one into Zion's pocket, right beside The Stone. She tucked one into her bosom. The third she slid across the table to Marcia.

Marcia looked at Zion, her eyes hard. "That stone protecting you, child. It is the Anchor. Keep the salt touching it. As long as the Anchor is on you, the water cannot touch what it protects."

"We keep the rules," Caro said, her voice steadying. "We hold the line."

Marcia took the salt. "We hold," she agreed. "But listen to the air, Caro. The digging outside... they are waking things that have been asleep a long time."

As if in answer, outside the front door, Patch scrambled to his feet and let out a single, deafening bark at the door. Not a warning. A challenge.

Zion clutched The Stone. The night was loud with the sound of his neighbors digging their own graves, and the only thing standing between the village and the rising tide was a boy, a dog, and three knots of salt.

CHAPTER 14
Samuel's Shadow

That night the house held its breath, but the village did not. Even after the digging stopped and the torches were doused, a manic energy hung over the lane. Laughter drifted from yards that should have been asleep. It was the sound of people drunk on relief, convinced they had broken the devil's back.

Inside, the air was thick enough to choke on. The humidity from the broken jars had seeped through the walls. The sheets felt damp; the wood of the table was slick to the touch.

Zion slept fitfully on his cot, The Stone clutched tight against his chest. His breathing deepened, then hitched, caught by a dream sent to find him through the thinning veil.

In the dream, Zion carried a small package wrapped in brown paper. It was heavy, heavier than lead, but the sender's voice had been clear: "Take it to Prospect. Cross the line, follow the trail, then keep left."

He walked an unfamiliar road. The iron rails of a railroad crossing gleamed under a moon that looked too bright. A low rumble in the distance warned of a train, but it never came. Zion hurried across the tracks and found the steep trail that rose beside a river.

The current below ran fast and hard, tearing white around great boulders. It was not the Lady's river; this water was angry, swirling deep in the hollows. The sound filled the air—wild, unbroken, alive.

The trail twisted upward, the river dropping away to his right until only its roar remained. It was dusk when the ground finally leveled, splitting at the edge of a village. A weathered board nailed to a cedar tree read: Prospect.

Zion turned left as instructed. The lane carried him past a small church with a lamp burning faintly in the window. Across the way a shop stood open, two people leaning at its counter, watching him with silent, hungry curiosity as he passed.

Soon he reached a house half-hidden in towering bamboo. The stalks swayed in the night wind, creaking and knocking, their hollow voices rising like whispers. Zion stopped at the gate, clutching the package. He called out, uncertain if dogs might rush from the dark.

The door opened. A man stepped into the yard squinting, a woman close behind, the lamplight spilling around them. The man's brow furrowed as he studied Zion. Then, slowly, his face softened, breaking into a smile that trembled at the edges. Tears welled in his eyes.

"My son," the man said, voice thick with a terrible joy. "You finally came."

Zion stiffened. He did not know this man.

"Come in," the man urged, pulling the gate wide. He turned to the woman beside him. "This is Lizzy. Your mother."

Her eyes were warm, reaching toward him, filled with a longing Zion could not name. The man's voice lowered, sounding like the river below. "You're home. We've waited so long for you."

The bamboo groaned in the wind. The river's roar rose again, swelling until it swallowed the words. Zion clutched the package tighter, feeling something inside it move, and the dream broke.

He woke with a gasp, sitting bolt upright. The Stone was pressed hard against his sternum, hot to the touch. Outside, Patch was barking—a rhythmic, monotonous warning directed at the dark.

~ ~ ~

Morning brought light, but it did not bring dryness.

Caro woke to find a thin film of moisture on the floorboards. When she went to the kitchen shelf to fetch the tin of salt, she found the lid stuck. She pried it open; the salt inside—the salt meant to protect them—had clumped into hard, damp stones.

She stared at it. The moisture wasn't just in the air; it was attacking their defenses.

Zion sat at the table, rubbing his eyes. He looked drained, as if he had walked miles in his sleep.

"Mama," he murmured. "I had a dream. I went to a place called Prospect."

Caro dropped the spoon. It clattered loudly in the basin. She turned slowly, her hands slick with the condensation on the bowl. "Prospect?"

"Yes. I crossed a railroad line. I walked up a steep trail by an angry river. A man was there. He said he was my father."

Caro felt the blood drain from her face. She pulled out a chair and sat down heavily. Her hands began to tremble.

"Tell me," she whispered, her voice cracking. "What did he look like?"

Zion frowned, digging into the memory. "Tall… and big shoulders. He smiled wide, but his eyes were sad, Mama. Like he was trapped in the yard."

Caro made a sound—half-sob, half-gasp. It was Samuel. The description was precise. The sadness in the eyes was something only she knew.

"He said a woman named Lizzy was my mother," Zion added. "He said they were waiting for me."

Caro stood up so fast the chair scraped violently against the floor.

"It's him," she said. She wasn't talking to Zion. She was talking to the air. "He's alive."

She rushed to the corner where the old chest sat. She threw the lid back. Her movements were frantic, clumsy. She grabbed a dress, Zion's good shirt, a pair of shoes.

"Mama?" Zion asked, scared. "What you doing?"

"We're going," Caro said, her voice high and breathless. "We're going to Prospect. I know the trail. I know the rail line at Morgans Pass."

She turned to Zion, her eyes wild.

"For thirteen years I thought he was bones in a gully," she cried, the words spilling out fast. "He went on a run for Elias and never came back. Everyone said Elias silenced him because he knew too much. We mourned him, Zion! We thought he was dead!"

She shoved the clothes into her market bag, her composure shattered.

"But my boy described him!" Caro moaned to herself. "The eyes, the smile! Elias didn't kill him. He kept him!"

Thirteen years of silence, thirteen years of assuming he was bones in a hole, and now the wound was ripped open. The strength she showed the village evaporated. She was just a woman who wanted her love back.

Marcia came out of the back room. She looked gray, her breathing shallow, but her eyes snapped to the bag in Caro's hand.

"Put it down," Marcia rasped.

"He's alive, Marcia!" Caro turned, tears streaming down her face. "Zion described him! The eyes, the smile! Elias didn't kill him. He kept him!"

"And now he wants you to come get him," Marcia said, stepping between Caro and the door. "Think, Caro. Why now? Why send the address in a dream when the village is digging up the jars?"

"I don't care why!" Caro tried to push past, but Marcia gripped her arm. Her fingers were weak, but her grip was desperate. "If he is there, I have to go. He is Zion's father!"

"He is bait!" Marcia shouted.

The word hung in the damp air.

"Elias is losing," Marcia said, breathing hard. "He is fighting a war on two fronts. Outside, the village is tearing down his walls—and he is letting them. He needs them to keep digging. It's a gamble; the digging weakens the very foundation he's bound to, but it's the fear behind the shovels that he's feeding on. He's drinking their panic just to maintain his hold."

She gripped Caro's arm, her eyes wide with the horror of the math. "The more they dig, the more the 'Science' bleeds out, but the stronger his grip gets on the shadows. He is trading his home for a weapon. And he knows you are the danger. The village is just noise and dirt, but you are the only one awake. You are the only one who can see the hand that's really holding the knife."

Caro was shaking, clutching the bag to her chest like a shield. "So I should leave him there? Trapped?"

"If you leave," Marcia said, her voice dropping to a harsh whisper, "you take the boy to a place where the river is angry. A place where you have no friends. And you leave this village to the Pastor and the mud."

Marcia pointed out the window. The sound of the crusade was starting up again—shouts, laughter, shovels hitting earth.

"Elias is dangling Samuel because he is scared of you," Marcia pressed. "He wants you to chase a ghost in the hills so you stop fighting the flood here. If you walk out that door, Elias wins. And Samuel stays trapped anyway."

Caro stared at Marcia, then at Zion, who was watching her with wide, terrified eyes. He had never seen his mother like this—unraveled.

Slowly, the fight drained out of her. The market bag slipped from her fingers and hit the floor.

She sank onto the chest, burying her face in her hands. "He showed him to me," she sobbed, her voice muffled. "He used my son's eyes to show me he is still suffering."

Marcia limped over and placed a hand on Caro's shoulder, her grip firm.

"He showed you a face, Caro," Marcia said, her voice hard with warning. "But we don't know what lies behind it. Maybe it is a man. Maybe it is only a memory Elias polished up to catch your eye."

She looked at the market bag on the floor.

"Dead or alive, the trap is the same," she whispered. "Elias doesn't need a man to be whole to make him dance. He only needs a thread. And right now, he is pulling on yours."

Caro looked up. Her eyes were red, raw with a grief that had turned into something sharper. "He thinks that's a lure," she whispered, wiping her face with a fierce, trembling hand. "He thinks I'll run into the hills and get lost."

She stood up. She didn't pick up the bag.

"I'm not going to Prospect," she said, though her voice shook. "Not today. But if he is holding Samuel... then I am going to break every jar in this valley until I find the one that holds his leash."

Marcia nodded, though her eyes remained worried. She saw the crack in Caro's armor. She knew that the next time Elias showed her Samuel, it might not be in a dream—and Caro might not be strong enough to stop.

"Good," Marcia said quietly. "Because the Pastor just rang the bell. The hunt is starting again."

Chapter 15
Caro's Stand

The rot moved faster than the clock.

By midday, the dampness that had started as a film on the floorboards had turned aggressive. In the kitchens along the lane, bread bought yesterday bloomed with green spots. Bananas on the table turned black in an hour, soft and weeping inside their skins.

The village was sick, but the village was too busy to notice.

Caro walked down the center of the road, her boots heavy with mud that shouldn't have been there. The dust of the dry season was gone, replaced by a greasy, slick paste that sucked at her heels. The air tasted of sulfur and deep, stagnant pools.

She passed Mr. Chin's shop. The shutters were half-closed, the wood swollen in the frames. On the porch, three men sat nursing white rum, their skin sheened with a sweat that didn't evaporate. They were coughing—wet, rattling coughs that sounded like water in a lung—but their eyes were bright, feverish with the gold rush of the crusade.

"Afternoon, Sister Caro," one called out, his voice raspy. "You join the harvest yet?"

"The harvest is rotting the fruit, Basil," Caro said, stopping. She pointed to his hand. The knuckles were swollen, the skin gray and puffy. "Look at you. You sick, and you don't even feel it."

Basil laughed, a sound that ended in a wheeze. "It just the night air, Caro. The Pastor say it's the body purging the old weakness. Making room for the new strength."

Caro tightened her grip on her bag. Purging. That was the word Williams had given them. A holy word for a dying symptom.

She walked on. She wasn't going to the fields. She was going to the source.

~ ~ ~

The churchyard was no longer a place of rest; it was a staging ground.

A mound of earth had been piled near the vestry door— the spoil from the morning's digging. And in the center of the yard, on a folding table usually reserved for harvest festivals and domino tournaments, sat the catch.

Twelve jars.

They were lined up like soldiers. Some were small, old medicine bottles turned opaque with time. Others were large pickling jars, their contents hidden behind glass that had gone purple in the earth. They didn't reflect the sun; they seemed to swallow the light.

A crowd of thirty or so had gathered, a mix of the curious and the devout. They stood in a loose circle, keeping a respectful distance from the table, whispering.

Patch, who had followed Caro against her orders, stopped at the gate. He lowered his head, his hackles rising in a jagged ridge. He let out a low, vibrating growl that he refused to swallow.

"Stay," Caro commanded.

THE COVENANT OF GLASS

She pushed through the gate. The air inside the yard was five degrees cooler than the road, a sudden, clammy drop that made the skin on her arms prickle.

Pastor Williams stood by the table. He looked wrecked and radiant. His white shirt was stained brown at the cuffs and hem, and he had tied a handkerchief around his forehead to catch the sweat that poured from him. He was vibrating, shifting his weight from foot to foot, his eyes scanning the crowd, scanning the sky, scanning a horizon only he could see.

"Pastor," Caro called out. Her voice was sharp, cutting through the murmurs of the crowd.

Williams turned. His smile was immediate, wide, and terrifyingly vacant.

"Sister Caro," he boomed. He spread his arms, and for a second, Caro saw the shadow of the man he used to be—the humble man who just wanted to fill the pews. That man was gone. "You have come to witness the liberation."

"I come to ask you to stop," Caro said. She walked until she was ten feet from him. The smell coming off the table was distinct—it smelled of copper and sour river-weeds, the kind that rot beneath a stone where the sun never reaches.

The crowd quieted. Sister Etta stepped forward, her face hard. "Mind your mouth, Caro. The Spirit moving."

"The Spirit don't smell like a swamp, Etta," Caro snapped, not looking at her. She kept her eyes on Williams. "Look at them, Thomas. Look at the children."

She pointed to a young girl holding her mother's skirt. The child's face was flushed, her breathing shallow and labored. "The village is burning up with fever... You are digging holes in the dam! Marcia told me the rules—if you break the glass in the dry, the rot has nowhere to go but into our lungs! You are poisoning the air because you are too lazy to walk to the river!"

Williams's smile didn't falter, but his eyes narrowed. "You are afraid," he said softly. "Fear is natural, sister. When the walls of Jericho fell, there was dust. There was noise. Change is a violent thing."

"This isn't change," Caro said, her voice rising. "It's suicide. Marcia told you—these jars are corks. They holding back the river. You break them, and the water takes us."

"Marcia Brown," Williams spat the name, his benevolence vanishing instantly. "Marcia Brown is the jailer! She and Elias, keeping the souls bound for twenty years! And you stand with them?"

He turned to the crowd, his voice pitching up, hitting that resonant frequency that made chests vibrate.

"Hear that?" he shouted. "She wants the jars to stay buried! She wants your blessings to stay in the ground! Why? Because she thinks you aren't strong enough to hold them!"

The crowd grumbled. It was a dark, ugly sound. Caro felt the shift in the air. They didn't see a concerned neighbor anymore; they saw an obstacle to their salvation.

"I don't want to keep nothing," Caro said, trying to keep her voice steady, though her heart hammered against her ribs. "I want us to live. Thomas, you having dreams. I know you are. But dreams can lie. The devil can dress up as an angel of light."

Williams laughed. It was a harsh, barking sound.

"The devil?" He reached out and picked up one of the jars —a heavy, square bottle sealed with red wax. He held it high. "You think the devil wants us to be free? I hear them, Caro! I hear the voices in the glass!"

He closed his eyes, tilting his head back.

"They are singing," he whispered, and the crowd leaned in, mesmerized. "They are in a stadium. Thousands of them. Roaring. Cheering. Waiting for the gate to open so they can fill this church. Fill this valley!"

He opened his eyes, and they were black with adrenaline.

"You hear a flood," he said to Caro. "I hear a congregation."

"It's water!" Caro screamed, desperate now. "It's the roar of water, you fool!"

Williams's face hardened into stone.

"Get thee behind me," he intoned.

He looked at the crowd. "She wants to stop the work. She wants to keep the captives in chains. What do we say to that?"

"Break it!" Etta shouted.

"Break it!" the man named Basil yelled, coughing into his fist.

"Break them all!" the crowd roared.

Williams looked at Caro with a pity that was worse than hate. "Watch, sister. Watch and be ashamed."

He raised the square bottle. He didn't use a hammer. He smashed it down onto the edge of the table.

CRACK.

The sound was like a gunshot. The glass exploded.

Caro flinched, throwing her arm up to shield her face.

There was no smoke. There was no ghost. But the air in the churchyard dropped. The pressure slammed down, popping ears. A sudden, violent gust of wind swirled from the center of the table—cold, wet wind that smelled of the deep ocean. It knocked the folding table sideways. It blew the handkerchief off Williams's head.

And from the shattered glass on the ground, a liquid oozed out. It wasn't wine or oil. It was muddy water, thick and dark, and it didn't soak into the dry dust. It pooled, bubbling, expanding faster than a cup of water should.

The crowd gasped, stumbling back.

"See!" Williams screamed, his arms raised to the wind, his shirt flapping wildly. "The breath of the Lord! He is blowing the chaff away!"

The water on the ground touched his shoe. He didn't move. He stood in the puddle, laughing, while the wind tore at the trees.

Caro backed away. She saw what they couldn't see. She saw the shadows stretching long and thin from the treeline, reaching toward the water. She saw the sickness on their faces deepening as the damp air rushed into their lungs.

They were cheering. They were clapping. Etta was dancing in the dirt, her feet stomping in the mud that was spreading from the broken jar.

Caro turned and ran.

She ran through the gate, past a growling Patch, and didn't stop until she reached the lane.

Zion was waiting there, pressed against the fence, his eyes wide. He had heard the smash. He felt the wave of cold air hit him.

"Mama?" he whispered.

Caro grabbed his arm, her grip bruising. Her face was pale, her eyes hard and dry. The sadness was gone. Only the terror remained, cold and clear.

"Get inside," she ordered, her voice shaking with a rage that had nowhere to go. "Board up the windows. Put the salt on the sills."

"Mama, what happen?"

Caro looked back at the churchyard, where the sound of singing was rising, competing with the unnatural wind.

"He is deaf," she said. "He is listening to the roar of his own drowning, and he thinks it is applause."

She shoved Zion toward the house.

"We lock the door," she whispered. "The damp is getting in. We have to hold the line until the fever breaks."

CHAPTER 16
Samuel Appears to Caro

The dream would not leave her.

Days after Zion spoke of Samuel, Caro found it rising into her thoughts at every idle moment—while she boiled yam, while she bent to tie a shoe, while her hands floated in the wash basin so long the water went cool. She could not forget the way the boy had said it: the railroad line, the steep trail by the river, the bamboo yards, and a man whose eyes smiled before his mouth did. Samuel's eyes.

She told herself it was only a child's dream. But the pictures would not fade. At night she lay awake and felt the river inside her chest, a steady pull she could neither soothe nor ignore. By morning the world looked the same, yet her mind kept tilting toward the hills as if the story might walk down the road and stand in her door.

She said little. To Zion she was brisk and gentle; to the women at the standpipe, polite; to herself, silent. Once, as Marcia sorted dried leaves into small paper twists, Caro said only, "It won't leave me." Marcia's hands paused, then moved again.

"Some dreams come with roots," she murmured, not looking up. "They hold fast till you pull the right thing."

Caro did not ask what that right thing might be. She did not trust her voice.

~ ~ ~

The afternoon it happened, the day wore a high hard light. Shadows lay thin as cloth across the lane. Patch dozed under the step, one paw twitching in a private chase, and Zion, who had helped haul water, had fallen asleep with his cheek pressed to the tabletop and The Stone cupped in his hand. The house made small, companionable sounds: oil settling in the lamp, a spoon tipping and righting itself in a cup.

Caro needed some ackee. She crossed the yard, lifted her basket, and stepped into the sun, heading toward the tree.

She saw him at once.

He stood at the far end of the lane, not facing her, his head slightly bent as if listening to something in the dust. Broad shoulders. The particular lift of the left one when he walked. Thirteen years fell away in a single breath. Her body knew the shape before her mind fastened a name.

Samuel.

Her heart knocked once, painfully. She told herself to call out—but the name caught. She told herself to stand still—but her legs carried her forward. He turned his head a fraction. The angle of his jaw, even in profile, was a blow.

As Caro stepped out of the yard, Patch's sudden barking split the air—sharp, insistent, almost frantic. He bounded to the path, hackles raised, blocking her way.

"Move, Patch," she hissed, trying to push past. But the dog stood firm, teeth bared at the path ahead, as if warning her.

She skirted him, her steps quickening past the old tamarind tree. Behind her, Patch's barking followed, echoing through the lane long after she'd turned the corner.

He had started down the path that led toward the river bend. He moved quickly—not a run, but the walk of a man with purpose, and not much time. Caro set her basket down under the tamarind tree and followed.

They passed low fences patched with tin, a goat nosing at a length of rope, a child asleep on a mat in the shade. Caro kept her steps measured, unwilling to startle him, unwilling to break the thin thread pulling her on. Twice she meant to speak his name, and twice she swallowed it. She needed to see his face.

At the corner he glanced back. For one narrow heartbeat she saw him fully. Older. Thinner in the cheek. But Samuel, unmistakable. And in his eyes a brightness she could not read —sorrow, maybe, or shame. The look caught at something deep in her that had never quite healed. He looked away quickly and lengthened his stride.

"Samuel—" The word scraped her throat and died.

The river came up on them suddenly, the path falling away to the bank. The water ran high, shouldering around black stones, speaking in a tongue of foam and hiss. He took it as a road, stepping onto slick rock with a surety that looked like memory. He did not test with his toes, did not spread his arms for balance, only moved from stone to stone, a clean, practiced crossing.

He reached midstream and turned. His trousers were wet to the knee. The sorrow in his eyes deepened, and his mouth shaped two words: forgive me.

Then he went on, three quick steps, and climbed the far bank. Bush leaned to swallow him.

Caro slid down the mud and into the shallows before she could think. The water was like prickly cold hands against her legs. Stones shifted underfoot, round as slippery, the rush of water making it twice as treacherous. The river spoke louder here, a shove of sound that rattled her ribs. She set her foot and moved, set and moved, eyes fixed on the place he had disappeared. The current pressed at her thighs. She had crossed this bend a hundred times as a girl, light and sure. But the river was hungrier today.

Halfway out, a lace of algae slicked beneath her heel. Her foot went sideways. For one absurd instant she was a woman in a house, arms flung to catch a falling pot. Then the river took her.

It seized and turned her, plunged her hard into a hollow she had forgotten hid there. Water closed over her head. The world narrowed to green-brown rush and the hot bloom of pain as her hip struck stone. She fought up and broke the surface gasping, turned toward the bank, and the current spun her like a leaf. She reached for anything and caught nothing. Her lungs crushed in her chest. She sank.

Something moved in the water with her.

It wasn't a thing she could see, only the shape of a laugh, oily and low, rising and falling with the river as if it breathed. A voice slid under the noise and wrapped the word around her like a chain: Doorway.

Her mind skittered. She had heard that voice in Zion's telling — the oily, mocking hunger beneath the words. Now it wrapped itself around her, cold and real, pulling her down. She clawed toward the surface. She could not find it. The laugh curled closer. Cold touched her scalp as though a hand brushed her hair, tender and terrible.

She thought, simply, Is this how I end—chasing ghosts?

Then hands took hold of her. Real. Human. Her head broke the skin of the river into air and light and noise. She coughed once, twice, seized with a spasm that wrung water from her. The hands hauled her backward, stumbling, dragging, until mud sucked at her heels and she collapsed on sand that felt hot as a stove.

"Miss Caro! You all right? You trying to kill yourself?"

She turned onto her side and saw Caleb Dawes—the man who lived across the valley—leaning over her, water dripping from his sleeves, face tight with alarm. He had come from upstream, a coil of rope looped over one shoulder, his boots already full.

"The rock there wicked," he said, breathless and half angry. "You don't cross alone when it running so."

Caro could not speak. She turned her face toward the opposite bank. Nothing moved there but bamboo, tall and close, knocking their hollow voices together in the wind. The place where Samuel had stood was only air and brush.

Caleb put a hand to her shoulder, awkward and gentle. "You can stand?"

She nodded, though the nod set the world tilting. He helped her up, steadying her while the river made the ground look as if it still moved. She thanked him when she found her breath. He shook his head.

"Give it a week and you laugh at it," he said roughly, trying to soften what had nearly happened. "Come. Let me walk you to the path."

They went slow to the almond tree. When he turned back upriver, he glanced once over his shoulder at the far bank, as if the bush itself bore watching. Then he was gone, his figure folding into light and leaf.

Caro stood with her hands on her knees until the shaking left her legs. The place where Samuel had looked at her—sorrow pooled in his eyes, mouth shaping forgiveness he could not give—held like a bruise at the center of her chest. At last she lifted her basket and walked home dripping, each step heavier than it should have been.

~ ~ ~

By evening the house had regained its small sounds. The lamp hissed. Patch lay with his head on his paws exactly in the line of the doorway, as if he had appointed himself the hinge between inside and out. Zion, worn from the heat and the morning's errands, had fallen asleep with The Stone in his palm, his fist closed like a bud. The sight steadied Caro more than she would ever say.

Marcia sat at the table with a little knife and a handful of dried leaves, trimming the stems as if peace could be made leaf by leaf. She looked up when Caro came in changed and dry, the damp of her hair tied back with a rag.

"You see him," Marcia said quietly. It was not a question.

Caro told it all because lies would have no power here: the first glimpse in the lane, the second near the bend, the eyes that met hers and flinched, the words he shaped across the water, the fall, the hole, the laugh in the river that was not a laugh, Caleb's hands pulling her back to air. She left nothing out, not even the part where she had wanted to call his name and could not.

Marcia listened the way a woman listens for weather, chin bowed, eyes steady. When Caro finished, she put down the knife and pressed her scarred wrist against the tabletop. The skin there, puckered into a pale cross, seemed to feel the story as if it were a hand laid on it.

"To me," she said at last, slow, "it sound like Elias playing you close now. He know your soft place. Him take the shape you would follow, and him set it on the far side of danger."

Caro's fingers curled on the table. "It was him," she said, too quickly, and tasted the need in the words. "It was Samuel. I saw it in the way he moved."

Marcia's mouth tightened, not in scorn but in caution. "Maybe so. Or maybe what Elias put on him like a coat. Hear me. Distance don't break a binding. If a man have a jar in Elias hand, Elias hold him from any road he walk. Kingston or Prospect. River or hill. Only the breaking of the jar cut the cord."

Caro stared at the scar, at the small rise and fall of it as Marcia's pulse beat beneath. "Do you think—" She could not finish the question.

Marcia's eyes lifted. She chose her words as if stepping from stone to stone herself. "I think it possible, yes. I think him clever enough to plant a man far and feed his reach with what he catch here. I think him short of strength now, and the shortest path back to it is your fear."

"So he came for me." Caro meant to make it a statement, and instead it broke.

Marcia's palm—cool, steady—touched the back of Caro's hand. "Him send the shadow first. That's how him test the door."

They sat for a while in the hum of the lamp. Outside, someone called a child home, the voice carrying sweet and ordinary along the lane. The ordinariness of it made Caro's throat ache.

At last she said, almost to herself, "He looked at me and asked forgiveness—as if he had chosen this. But if what you say is true, there was no choosing."

Marcia did not answer, because there are some knots that only time will loosen. Instead she reached to the little pinch of salt wrapped in cloth she kept tied at her waist and set it there between them.

"We keep the rules," she said, voice steadying to work. "We hold the boy to them. Salt on the thresholds. The Stone stays on his skin, never hid away. And if a jar comes to hand, you know where it must go. We make small ground where Elias's foot can't settle."

Caro nodded. Work steadied her more than comfort. "And the Pastor," she said, the word dry as old wood. "We still find his jar first."

Marcia's gaze dropped to her scar again. "That one will cut deep. But we cannot break it here. We must carry it to the water and break it in the current. It will sever his cord."

"Then we take it to the water," Caro said, her voice hard. "And we let him howl."

From the cot, Zion turned and pulled the sheet close. The Stone shifted in his fist, a small shape against his palm. Patch lifted his head, ears angling toward the door, then lay down again with a sigh that stirred the dust.

Caro rose and crossed to the basin. She washed her hands as if the river were still on them and dried them slow. When she came back to the table, she did not sit. She laid her hand light on Marcia's shoulder.

"Thank you," she said. The words were plain and all she had.

Marcia covered Caro's hand with her own. "We not done yet."

"No," Caro said. She looked toward the open door, toward the part of the yard where a man had stood in her memory and shaped an apology over water. "We are not."

Later, when the lamp was turned down to a thin blue wick and the yard held its breath between late and later, Caro lay on the bed with Zion's steady breathing a comfort in the dark. Her mind went back, not to the fall, not to the laugh, but to the small, sharp look that had crossed Samuel's face when he turned his head—not joy exactly, not fear, but the knowledge of a debt that had come home. She let that look fix in her like a nail.

The path ahead felt narrow as a ridge. But a plan—fragile, dangerous—had begun to gather its edges: find the tether that held the Pastor, then the one that might still hold Samuel. Break what fed Elias. Starve his reach. If he came at her through love, then she would answer him with ruin.

She closed her eyes and did not sleep for a long time. The river moved in its bed beyond the bend, shouldering past rocks, keeping its own counsel. Inside the little house, the boy held a stone meant to keep shut what must not be let loose, and the women at the table kept the shape of their courage small and clean and ready.

CHAPTER 17

The Fire and the Water

The dampness had a sound now.

It wasn't just the wet slick on the walls or the mildew blooming on the Sunday bests hanging in wardrobes. It was a low groan beneath the earth, like a stomach digesting a heavy meal.

Inside the Community Hall, the air was close enough to strangle. The hall, a wooden structure that leaned tiredly against the back of the church, was packed. Pastor Williams had called for a "Vigil of Breaking"—a night to pray down the remaining strongholds.

Zion sat near the back door, wedged between Caro and the wall. The Stone in his pocket was so cold it numbed his thigh, a freezing point in a room boiling with heat.

"Look at them," Caro whispered, her mouth close to his ear. "Drunk on it."

She was right. The village wasn't just praying; they were swaying in a fever dream. The kerosene lamps hung from the rafters, casting long, swinging shadows that made the congregation look like a single, heaving organism. Men who usually sat stoic in the back pews were now shouting "Yes, Lord!" and "Break it down!" Women were weeping, their faces shiny with sweat that refused to dry.

At the front, Pastor Williams paced the stage. The mud from the jar he had broken days ago still stained his shoes, but he hadn't cleaned them. He wore the dirt like a vestment.

"The enemy tries to suffocate us!" he roared, his voice hoarse. He pointed to the ceiling, where condensation was gathering on the zinc sheets and dripping down like slow rain. "He sends the heavy air to weigh us down! But what does the fire do?"

"Burn!" Sister Etta shrieked from the front row. She was rocking back and forth, eyes rolled back, a tambourine trembling in her hand.

"The fire consumes!" Williams shouted. "We need the fire to dry out the damp! We need the Holy Ghost fire to burn the rot out of this valley!"

The crowd roared. It was a desperate sound. They were sick—Zion could hear the wet coughing rippling through the room like a chorus—but they believed the Pastor offered the cure. They believed that if they screamed loud enough, the mold would retreat.

It happened fast, born of exhaustion and hysteria.

Sister Etta, seized by a sudden convulsion of the spirit, threw her hands up. "Fire!" she screamed, spinning in a circle. "Send the fire!"

Her hand struck the stand of a kerosene lamp placed too close to the edge of the stage.

The lamp teetered. Time seemed to slow. Zion watched the glass chimney slide off, watched the metal base tip.

It hit the floorboards with a shatter. The oil sprayed out, not in a puddle, but in a fan. The wick, still burning, hit the oil.

Whump.

The flame didn't hesitate. It leaped up the dry, varnished wood of the stage skirting. It caught the hem of the table cloth. In seconds, a wall of orange heat roared up the front of the hall.

Panic is a contagious thing.

"Fire!" someone screamed, a different kind of scream this time.

The congregation scrambled backward, knocking over benches. The exit was blocked by the press of bodies. The heat was instantaneous, searing the already humid air.

Pastor Williams stood on the stage, backing away from the flames licking at his shoes. He looked confused, as if the metaphor he had summoned had suddenly decided to eat him.

"Water!" a man yelled. "Get the bucket!"

But there were no buckets. The fire climbed the curtains, reaching for the rafters. Smoke, black and oily, began to roll across the ceiling.

Zion coughed, burying his face in his shirt. Caro grabbed him, pulling him toward the window. "Out! We have to get out!"

Then, the floor screamed.

It wasn't the crackle of burning wood. It was the sound of wood snapping under immense pressure from below.

Right in the center of the hall, between the terrified crowd and the burning stage, the floorboards bowed upward. Nails popped with sounds like pistol shots.

CRACK.

The floor split open.

It wasn't a trickle. It was a geyser.

A column of water, thick and brown as chocolate, erupted from the earth. It smashed through the wood, hitting the ceiling with enough force to dent the zinc.

It exploded outward, drenching the front rows, drenching the Pastor, and—most importantly—smashing into the fire.

The water was violent. It hissed as it hit the flames, sending up a blinding cloud of white steam. The fire fought for a second, turning the steam gray, and then it died. Drowned.

The geyser subsided as quickly as it had burst, settling into a bubbling, aggressive flow that gurgled up through the shattered floorboards.

Silence fell over the hall. The only sound was the glug-glug-glug of water rising and the hiss of cooling embers.

The steam cleared. The stage was blackened and charred, but the fire was out.

The floor was gone. In its place was a pool of muddy water, swirling with debris, expanding outward, soaking the shoes of the faithful.

Pastor Williams stood on the sodden stage. He was dripping wet. His white shirt clung to his skin, translucent.

He looked at the hole in the floor. He looked at the water bubbling up, dark and smelling of the river bottom.

A sane man would have seen a broken main or a flash flood. But Thomas Williams had not been a sane man since the night of the stadium dream.

He began to laugh.

It started as a giggle and rose to a shout. He fell to his knees in the mud on the stage, splashing the black water over his face.

"A miracle!" he screamed.

The crowd, huddled against the back walls, stared at him.

"The Lord has answered!" Williams cried, pointing to the geyser. "We asked for fire, but He knew we needed the water! He has struck the rock! He has sent the river of Jordan to spring up in His house to save us!"

He looked at them, his eyes wild. "Don't you see? The earth is giving up its dead! The blessings are flowing up!"

"Hallelujah," Etta whispered, shivering in the cold steam. She stepped forward, tentatively, and let the muddy water wash over her feet. "It warm. It warm like blood."

"It's a sign!" another voice shouted.

The fear in the room broke, replaced by a delirious, sobbing relief. They hadn't burned. Therefore, they were saved. Therefore, the water was good.

Caro did not move. She stood by the window, holding Zion's shoulder. Her grip was iron.

She looked at the water. It wasn't receding. It was rising. The level was inching up the table legs.

"Come," she whispered to Zion.

They slipped out the back door while the village began to sing a hymn of thanksgiving to the mud.

~ ~ ~

Outside, the night air felt thin compared to the steam bath of the hall. Patch was waiting for them, pacing in circles, whining at the ground.

Marcia was there too. She was standing by the corner of the church, her hand pressed against the foundation stones.

"You see it?" Marcia asked, not turning around.

"I saw it," Caro said. "The fire start, and the ground vomit up the water to stop it."

"The Pastor say it's a miracle," Zion said, his voice trembling. "He say God send the Jordan."

Marcia turned. Her face was grim in the moonlight.

"That is no Jordan," she said. "The jars, Zion. They are the corks in the bottle. The village break so many now that the pressure is too high."

She pointed to the ground.

"The water table rising," she said. "The river isn't in its bed anymore. It is under the village. It is looking for every weak spot to push through."

Caro looked back at the hall. The singing was loud now, drowning out the sound of the bubbling floor.

"They are dancing in it," Caro said, appalled. "They are washing themselves in the flood."

"Let them dance," Marcia said, her voice dropping to a whisper. "But you watch the ground in your own yard. Because once the water finds a door, it don't leave."

Zion put his hand in his pocket. The Stone was no longer cold. It was vibrating, a low, steady hum that matched the groan of the earth.

"She coming," Zion whispered.

Both women looked at him.

"Who?" Caro asked.

Zion looked toward the river, hidden in the dark.

"The Lady," he said. "She's not waiting for the rain. She's coming up through the floor."

CHAPTER 18
The Silent Anchor

The morning after the fire, the birds did not sing.

It was the first thing Zion noticed when he stepped outside the. Usually, the mango tree was alive with ground-doves and kling-klings, their black bodies squabbling and dive-bombing for the sweetest fallen fruit. Today, the branches were empty. The air was still and heavy, pressing against his eardrums like he was deep underwater.

Inside the house, Caro and Marcia were speaking in low, frantic tones, mapping out where the Pastor might go next. Zion didn't want to hear it. He felt a pull in his chest, a physical tug that had nothing to do with the argument in the kitchen.

THE COVENANT OF GLASS

He slipped through the gate. Patch was there, lying in the dust. The dog looked up, his eyes rimmed with red, and whined. When Zion started toward the trail that led to the river, Patch stood up, took three steps, and then stopped. He barked once, lowered his head, and refused to go further.

Zion went alone.

~ ~ ~

The path down to the water was slick. The mud here didn't dry anymore. The deeper he went into the bush, the colder it got. It wasn't a clean, breezy cold; it was the damp chill of a cellar that hasn't been opened in years.

He reached the break in the cane where the river usually came into view. He stopped, confused.

The river was wrong.

Usually, the river chatted. It slapped against the rocks, hissed over the shallows, and gurgled in the eddies. Even in flood, it roared.

But today, there was no sound.

Zion stepped out onto the bank. The water was shockingly high—swollen, brown, and muscular. It had swallowed the white stones where the women did their washing. It had climbed past the tree roots. It moved with a terrifying, oily speed, sliding past the village like a massive, liquid snake.

It was silent because it was too deep to break over the rocks. It was just sheer, heavy volume, sliding on its journey.

Zion stood at the edge, his boots sinking into the saturated earth. He felt small. The river didn't look like water anymore; it looked like a living thing that was holding its breath.

He put his hand in his pocket. He needed something solid to hold onto. His fingers closed around the black Stone.

Thunk.

His knees buckled.

The moment he touched The Stone near the water, its weight changed. It didn't grow larger, but it suddenly felt as heavy as a cannonball. It dragged his hand down, pulling his arm straight, anchoring him to the spot.

Zion gasped, trying to lift it, but The Stone wanted to be down. It wanted to be near the earth.

He looked at the rushing brown water. A whirlpool spun slowly near the bank, a dark, hungry eye that seemed to be watching him. The current whispered, a low vibration that he felt in his teeth rather than heard.

Let go, the silence seemed to say. It's easier to float.

He felt a sudden, dizzying urge to step forward. The water looked soft. It looked like it would wash away the heat, the rot, the Pastor's shouting, and his mother's fear. Just one step.

He leaned toward the edge.

The Stone flared cold in his hand—ice cold. The weight of it jerked him back, physically pinning him to the mud.

Zion stumbled backward, his heart hammering. He looked at the black rock in his palm.

For weeks, he had thought it was a weapon. He had imagined throwing it at Elias, cracking the ghost's skull like a Goliath.

But as he stood trembling on the bank, he understood. You don't throw this.

It's an anchor, he realized. It's the only thing heavy enough to keep you from washing away.

He looked upriver, toward the bridge, and then downriver, toward the cane fields.

Up on the hill, the air still smelled of wet ash, but the singing had stopped. The ruins of the Community Hall were quiet. The village was sleeping off the exhaustion of the fire, believing the "miracle" water had saved them. They were resting in their beds, convinced the war was over.

Zion looked down at the brown water, inches from overflowing the bank.

They weren't fighting spirits. They were fighting gravity.

Elias had spent twenty years tying the river down with knots and glass. Now the knots were cut. The river wasn't angry; it was just loose. And the sleeping village was sitting right in its path.

A dead branch floated past. It was massive, a whole log, moving fast. It struck a submerged rock with a dull, heavy thud—the only sound in the valley—and then vanished under the brown surface.

That was the village. That log was the church.

Zion shoved the heavy stone deep into his pocket, fighting the urge to run, forcing himself to walk backward until he was safe in the trees. Only then did he turn and sprint.

~ ~ ~

He burst into the kitchen, breathless, his boots leaving dark, wet streaks on the floor. The room smelled of stale coffee and sleeplessness.

Caro jumped up from the stove. "Zion? Where you go? I tell you to stay in the yard!"

Zion ignored her. He looked at Marcia. She was sitting at the table, her hands still, her eyes tracking him. She looked as tired as the house felt.

"The Pastor thinks it's a war," Zion panted, clutching The Stone through the fabric of his pocket. "He thinks he is fighting the devil."

"He is fighting his own shadow," Marcia said quietly.

"No," Zion said.

He looked up, and his eyes were suddenly clear, emptied of fear. The hum of The Stone seemed to vibrate in his voice, making Caro step back. It was the same cold authority she had heard the morning he exposed the village's sins.

"The River is finished with knots," The Prosecutor said. The voice was older than the boy's throat. "She is not angry. She is simply... arriving. The lease is up."

He looked at his mother. The boyish panic flickered back into his face for a second, then vanished under that cold, heavy stillness.

"The water isn't waiting for a spell, Mama. The Cork is loose. The debt collector is at the door."

Caro stared at him. The boy who had left the house an hour ago had been a frightened child. The boy standing there now looked like he had seen the end of the world and measured it.

"We have to find the jar," Zion said, his voice steady. "Not to save the Pastor. To keep the cork in."

Marcia nodded slowly, her fingers drumming a nervous rhythm on the wood. She recognized the tone. It was the truth. If that breaks, Elias feasts one last time. We starve him now."

"Then we best be quick," she said, looking toward the window where the sounds of the Pastor's digging crew were drifting down from the hill. "Because the fire gave Thomas a taste of power. And a man like that doesn't wait for Sunday to start the breaking."

CHAPTER 19
The Judas Jar

They were already too late.

Even as Marcia spoke the warning in the kitchen, the rhythm of the digging on the hill changed. The dull thud of shovels against wet earth ceased, replaced by a sharp, high-pitched chink. Glass against stone.

The discovery had begun in the grey, sweating hours of dawn, while the village was still sleeping off the exhaustion of the fire. The geyser in the Community Hall had stopped, leaving behind a crater of slick, black mud. But the water hadn't just destroyed the floor; it had washed away the earth beneath the foundation, opening a throat in the ground.

Pastor Williams had not gone home. He had spent the night wading in the muck, singing hymns under his breath, digging with his bare hands.

He found the first one as the sun rose.

By noon, the bell was ringing.

Zion heard the commotion from the road. It sounded like a celebration—shouts, clapping, the ringing of the church bell in short, sharp bursts.

"Stay here," Caro said, wiping her hands on a rag, though the dread on her face said she knew exactly what that sound meant.

"No," Zion said. He stood up from the step. He felt the heavy drag of The Stone in his pocket. He wasn't asking.

Caro looked at him, saw the new hardness in his jaw, and didn't argue. "Stay close to me, then."

~ ~ ~

They didn't go to the Hall. The crowd was gathered further down, where the land sloped sharply toward the riverbank.

The blowout from the geyser had eroded the soil, revealing the limestone ribs of the earth.

There, beneath the roots of a massive guango tree that anchored the churchyard, the earth had peeled away to reveal a hollow. It wasn't a natural cave. It was a dugout, reinforced with old railway sleepers and sealed with clay.

The villagers stood in a wide semi-circle, kept back by two deacons holding shovels. In the center, Pastor Williams was pulling them out.

They came out wet and gleaming. Jars. Hundreds of them.

They weren't like the scattered ones in the cane fields. These were uniform—heavy, dark glass, sealed with wax that had turned black with age. He stacked them in a pyramid on the grass. The sound of glass clinking against glass was delicate, musical, and terrifying.

"Look at them!" Williams shouted, his voice cracking with fatigue and triumph. He held up a large bottle, the size of a gas lantern. "The devil thought he could hide them under the Lord's house! But the water washed the covering away!"

He looked at the crowd, his eyes feverish.

"We have found the nest of vipers," he declared. "We have found the source of the curse."

Marcia appeared beside Caro. She moved silently, her cane sinking into the soft ground. She stared at the pyramid of glass with a look of sick recognition.

"The Foundation," she whispered.

"I don't understand," Caro said, voicing the question that hung in the air. "I thought the jars were in the cane fields. In the hut where he kept you. How did Elias move them all here?"

Marcia shook her head slowly.

"He didn't move them, Caro. They have been here since the beginning."

She pointed a trembling finger at the concrete slab of the church foundation visible above the hole.

"The hut was just the marketplace," Marcia rasped. "That was where he traded small things—a love spell here, a curse there. That was the daily bread I tended."

She looked at the massive pile of black glass.

"But this... this is the Bank. These are the Anchors. Twenty years ago, when Thomas broke ground for this sanctuary,

Elias told him the land needed 'preparation.' He told Thomas to bury these as cornerstones."

Zion frowned. "The Pastor knew?"

"He knew then," Marcia said. "But ambition is a blinding thing. Thomas let Elias bury the heavy debts here—the big sacrifices needed to stop the river the first time. Then Thomas poured the concrete over them and forgot."

"Forgot?" Caro asked. "How do you forget a graveyard under your feet?"

Marcia looked at the Pastor, who was stacking the black jars with the fervor of a man saving his flock. She shook her head, the memory eluding her for a moment.

"He wanted to forget, Caro," she said softly. "He built his church on a lie to hold the village together. He doesn't realize he is digging up his own bargain."

Williams was lifting another jar. This one was different.

It wasn't black glass. It was clear, but the inside was coated with silver paint, turning the vessel into a mirror. It caught the sun, flashing blindingly bright. The seal wasn't black wax; it was a heavy drip of shimmering silver wax, stamped with a coin.

Marcia drew in a sharp breath. The sound was like a hiss.

"What is it?" Zion asked.

"The Judas," Marcia whispered, the memory suddenly flooding back. "I haven't seen that bottle in twenty years. Elias kept it on his table."

She grabbed Caro's arm, her fingers digging in.

"That is the answer, Caro," she said urgently. "That is how he forgot."

She pointed a trembling finger at the silver vessel.

"You bottle the memory," she said, her voice shaking. "You take the part of you that knows it's a sin, and you seal it in silver. For twenty years, Thomas has walked on this floor believing he was holy, because his conscience was corked in that jar."

Caro watched the Pastor, who was cradling the silver jar against his chest, the sudden realization dawning. "Elias captured his conscience."

"Tomorrow!" Williams roared, turning to the crowd. "Tomorrow is Sunday! We will not break these in the dirt like thieves! We will bring them to the altar! We will have a Great

Cleansing! We will smash the head of the serpent before the eyes of God!"

The crowd cheered. It was a hungry, ragged sound.

"He's going to wait," Caro said, relief flooding her voice. "We have tonight."

"He is guarding them," Marcia noted.

She was right. Williams didn't put the silver jar down. He gestured to the deacons. "Watch the pile. No one touches it until the service. The devil will try to steal back his own."

~ ~ ~

Night fell, but the village didn't get dark. Torches burned around the guango tree. The Pastor had set a rotation of guards—men armed with machetes, singing hymns to keep themselves awake.

Inside Caro's house, the mood was surgical.

"We can't take them all," Marcia said, tracing a pattern on the table. "There are too many. But we need the Judas."

"We have to find the jar," Zion said, his voice steady. "Not to save the Pastor. To keep the cork in."

Marcia nodded slowly, her hollow eyes fixed on the distant church. "That jar was his lock, but now it is his last feast. If that guilt breaks, Elias gets the final rush of power he needs to fight the flood. We starve him now."

"And Samuel?" Caro asked. Her voice was steady, but her hands were clenched. "If his jar is in that pile..."

"We look for blue wax," Marcia said. "Elias marked the blood-debts with blue."

The plan was desperate. The guards were focused on the perimeter, facing the road. But the hollow opened toward the river.

"Zion is the smallest," Marcia said.

"No," Caro said immediately.

"He is the only one the dogs won't bark at," Marcia countered. "And he has the anchor."

Zion touched his pocket. The Stone was warm. "I can do it, Mama. I can go up the mud bank."

Caro looked at him. She looked at the window, where the orange glow of the torches flickered against the night sky. She realized, with a sinking heart, that she had run out of ways to protect him.

"You don't touch nothing but the silver one," Caro ordered, her voice tight. "And if you see blue wax... you tell me. You don't try to carry two. You hear?"

~ ~ ~

The river smell was overwhelming—a thick, cloying scent of vegetation and wet earth. Zion crawled up the slope from the water's edge. The mud was slick as grease. Below him, the silent river moved like a conveyor belt in the dark.

He reached the lip of the hollow.

The roots of the guango tree formed a cage around the stash. Through the gaps, he could see the pyramid of jars, glistening in the torchlight.

The guards were on the other side, facing the churchyard, talking in low voices about the fire and the miracle.

Zion squeezed between two roots. He was inside the cage.

The air in the hollow was freezing cold, despite the humid night. The jars radiated a chill that made his teeth ache. He scanned the pile.

Black wax. Black wax. Black wax.

Then he stopped. Near the bottom, tucked deep in the structural heart of the pyramid, he saw the color.

Blue wax.

But it wasn't just one.

Now that his eyes adjusted, he saw them everywhere—a vein of blue running through the black glass like a bruised artery. There were scores of them, too many to count. Blood debts. Big sacrifices.

Zion's heart hammered against his ribs. Which one?

Marcia had guessed. Caro was hoping. But looking at the tangled nest of glass, Zion realized the truth. To find Samuel, he would have to dismantle the whole bank. He would have to break the church to find his father.

He reached for the closest blue jar anyway—desperation moving his hand—but it was wedged tight under the crushing weight of a hundred others.

I can't save him tonight, he thought, the realization cold as the river water. Not without bringing the whole thing down.

He pulled his hand back. He had to stick to the mission. Where was the silver one?

He looked up.

It wasn't in the pile.

Zion shifted, peering through the roots toward the camp.

Pastor Williams was sitting on a folding chair right in front of the hoard. He was asleep, his head lolling on his chest. The silver jar—the Judas—was in his lap. His hands were clasped over the cork.

Zion froze. He felt The Stone in his pocket turn ice cold.

He didn't just see a sleeping man. In the silence, Zion heard the hum—a low, sick vibration passing from the silver glass into the Pastor's fingers. A conversation. The jar was singing a lullaby to the man's conscience, keeping him trapped in a dream of glory.

"He took the child's payment to bury the child's existence," Zion whispered, though the words did not come from his mouth. "A silver coin sealed in silver glass. The lie he told himself is the lullaby that keeps him asleep."

He is not holding it, Zion realized with a jolt of horror. It is holding him.

Zion slithered backward, inch by inch, sliding down the mud until he hit the riverbank. He scrambled away into the dark.

~ ~ ~

"Him holding it?" Marcia asked.

Zion stood by the table. He looked pale, shaken not by the guards, but by what he had felt in the hollow.

"He is fused to it," Zion whispered. "The silver glass... it eating him, Mama. I heard it feeding. If we try to take it, he will scream before he wakes."

Marcia's face went grim. She recognized the description. It was the same way Elias had bound her.

"The connection is too strong," Marcia said. "He will carry it to the pulpit."

"So we have to stop him in the church," Caro said.

"In front of everybody?" Zion asked. "They will kill us."

"Let them try," Caro said. She stood up and went to the drawer. She took out the long knife she used for cutting cane.

She didn't look like a mother anymore. She looked like a soldier at the end of a losing war.

"Tomorrow is Sunday," she said. "We go to service."

Outside, the church bell began to toll midnight.

It was the first time it had done that. Williams was sending a message: the day of reckoning had begun. It sounded heavy and dull, like a hammer hitting wet wood.

The river rose another inch. Sunday had arrived.

CHAPTER 20
The Breaking

Sunday morning did not dawn bright. The sun was there, somewhere behind a ceiling of bruised, purple clouds, but the light that filtered down was grey and diffuse. The air was so thick with moisture that breathing felt like drinking warm soup.

The church bell began to ring at eight. It sounded muffled, the iron tongue striking metal that had lost its resonance. Clung. Clung. Clung.

Inside the church, the atmosphere was manic.

Every pew was full. People stood in the aisles, pressed shoulder to shoulder, their Sunday whites already translucent with sweat. They fanned themselves with hymn books, a thousand fluttering wings that did nothing to move the heavy air.

But eyes were not on the cross. They were on the altar.

The pyramid of jars sat there, a dark, glassy monument rising almost to the pulpit. The "Nest" that Elias had hidden for twenty years was now the centerpiece of the sanctuary. It gleamed with a dull, oily sheen.

And right in the center, resting on the velvet cushion usually reserved for the Holy Bible, sat the Silver Jar.

~ ~ ~

Zion walked between Caro and Marcia. They moved up the side aisle, against the wall.

They were not dressed for church. Caro wore her work boots and a dark skirt, her market bag heavy on her shoulder. Marcia leaned hard on her cane, her face set in a grim mask. Zion kept his hand in his pocket, clutching The Stone until his knuckles ached.

Heads turned as they passed. The whispers were not kind.

"Look the jailer come." "She come to stop the blessing."

Sister Etta blocked their path near the third row. Her eyes were glazed, her body vibrating with a spiritual tremors.

"You have no business here, Marcia Brown," Etta hissed. "This is a place of light."

"This is a tomb, Etta," Marcia said... "And you are standing on the trapdoor. Are you all too blind to see what this church is built on? The Pastor is not blameless, yet you follow him into the dark."

She pushed past, her cane thumping on the floorboards. Etta shrank back, superstition warring with her fervor.

They found a spot near a pillar, twenty feet from the altar. It was close enough to rush, but far enough to see the whole stage.

Pastor Williams ascended the pulpit.

He looked terrible. He looked magnificent.

His eyes were sunken, rimmed with dark circles like bruises, but the pupils were dilated, swallowing the irises. He gripped the sides of the wooden podium as if he were steering a ship in a gale.

"They told us to wait!" he whispered.

His voice didn't need amplification. In the breathless, terrified silence of the sanctuary, the acoustics of the building carried his voice to the very back row like the hiss of a snake.

"For twenty years, they told us to wait. To be patient. To be poor."

He pointed a shaking finger at the pyramid of jars.

"But the Lord said: 'I have stored up the wealth of the sinner for the just!'"

"Amen!" the crowd roared. It wasn't a church Amen; it was the roar of a crowd that smells blood.

"They hid your joy in the dirt!" Williams screamed. "They hid your healing in the riverbank! But today... today we make the withdrawal!"

He stepped down from the pulpit. He walked to the altar and picked up the Silver Jar.

The room went silent. The only sound was the groan of the earth beneath the floorboards—slight subterranean pulses and constant, churning rumble that most mistook for the Holy Spirit moving.

Williams caressed the silver glass. He looked at it with a tenderness that made Zion's stomach turn.

"I hear you," Williams murmured to the jar. "You want to sing. You want to join the choir."

He raised his head. He looked straight at Marcia.

"The witch is here," Williams announced. The crowd turned, a sea of hostile faces. "She wants to keep the seals on. She wants to keep the heavy air over you."

He took a step toward them, holding the jar like a weapon.

Caro's hand went into her market bag. She gripped the handle of the cutlass just to be safe. Marcia reached and lightly held her other hand.

"Why, Marcia? Are you afraid of what will happen when the glory falls?"

"I am afraid of the water, Thomas," Marcia said. She didn't shout, but in the hush, her voice carried. "Put the bottle down. That isn't glory inside. It is your own leash."

Williams laughed. It was a wet, rattling sound.

"My leash? No. This is my freedom."

He turned back to the altar. He placed his hand on the stack, his fingers brushing a jar with blue wax.

"Samuel," Caro whispered. The name was a strangled sob.

She ripped her arm free from Marcia. She lunged into the aisle.

"Thomas, no!" Caro screamed, raising the knife.

The crowd gasped. Two deacons tackled her before she made three steps. They dragged her back, the cutlass skittering across the floor.

"Mama!" Zion shouted. He tried to run to her, but the press of bodies held him fast.

Williams didn't even flinch. He looked at Caro, pinned on the floor, and smiled. A sad, benevolent, insane smile.

"You see?" he said to the crowd. "They come with knives. We come with faith."

"Let us begin," Williams declared.

He didn't start with the blue jar. He didn't start with the small ones.

He lifted the Silver Jar—the Judas—high above his head.

"Open the gates!" he screamed. "Open the stadium!"

"Don't!" Zion yelled, his voice cracking. "It's a dam!"

Williams brought the jar down.

He smashed it, not on the floor, but right onto the apex of the pyramid of jars.

CRASH.

The sound was deafening. The silver jar shattered. The force of the blow drove shards into the jars beneath it. A chain reaction began. The pyramid collapsed in a cascade of breaking glass.

Smash. Tink. Crash.

A shattering cascade of glass broke at once, a sound that appeared to last for an eternity.

Then for one second, there was absolute silence.

A mist rose from the broken glass—a grey, swirling vapor that smelled of sulphur and ozone.

Then, the scream came.

It didn't come from the Pastor. It came from the air itself. A high, thinning wail that sounded like a man falling from a great height.

Elias.

A shape flickered in the grey mist—a tall, jagged shadow, frantic, terrified. He wasn't attacking. He was trying to run.

But the floor beneath the altar didn't just crack this time. It vanished.

BOOM.

The explosion knocked the front row of pews backward.

The earth beneath the altar blew out. It wasn't a geyser. It was a wall.

A solid slug of brown water, moving with the force of a freight train, punched up through the foundation.

It hit the shadow of Elias. The scream was cut off instantly. The ghost didn't fade; he was shattered—dispersed and forced to become one with the churning torrent by the sheer physical mass of the river.

The water hit the roof. The zinc sheets peeled back like paper.

Then gravity took over. The water came down.

It wasn't a splash. It was a deluge. The altar, the pulpit, the choir loft—they were simply erased.

Pastor Williams was standing there one second, his arms raised in victory. The next second, he was gone, swept backward into the congregation by a chest-high wave of mud, glass, and timber.

"Run!" Marcia screamed, shoving Zion.

But there was nowhere to run. The doors were blocked by the crush of people trying to escape.

The floor of the church began to tilt. The water wasn't just coming from the altar; it was coming through the walls. The "damp" had finally pushed through.

The river had arrived. The service was over.

PART 3
THE FLOOD

Chapter 21
The Stadium Realized

Twenty years before, The Lady felt the wrenching blow not as pain, but as an impossible, sickening silence.

The man, Elias, stood in the dry mud of her emptied riverbed, his hands smeared with a mixture of salt and wax. He did not speak. He was following the dark rules he had found in a book from another land: To quiet the Fluid Spirit, one must first remove the Pulse.

He knelt where the water had once gathered deep and lifted the Anchor—the black stone that was the slow, steady heart of the earth and the rhythm of the current.

The Lady watched from the shadows of the remaining pool. She was the fluid spirit, a force of water and will. The Stone was pure, solid earth. She understood the law immediately: Elias, being flesh and earthbound, could lift The Stone; she, being spirit, could only rage against the space where it had been.

He wrapped The Stone in oilcloth and walked away to hide it on the high ground, satisfied.

The Lady did not weep or curse. She simply waited. Her memory was eternal, deeper than any ocean, and she understood the nature of his theft. The man thought he had stolen the heart of the river. But a heart does not die; it waits for a pulse.

The rules were simple:

The spirit cannot touch the earth.

The binding is held in place by the debt of the flesh.

Therefore, only a hand of flesh could return the heart.

She withdrew to the deepest part of the current. Her power could not lift The Stone, but her consciousness could direct the water. For twenty years, she would use the leaking current to slowly guide The Stone to the edge of the bank. She would spend twenty years weakening the spiritual walls of his dam—the jars—until a crack appeared.

And she would wait for the right hand to be born and come to her.

She waited for a child without debt. A soul so clean that the stolen Stone would gravitate to him, and Elias's power could not claim him. She waited for the only hand that could complete the journey. And when the boy came, she would use the water like a glove to push The Stone from her realm to his, completing the transfer without violating the natural laws.

~ ~ ~

The roar was the first thing that killed the hope.

For weeks, Pastor Williams had preached about the sound of the stadium—the cheering of saved souls, the applause of heaven. As the water blew the roof off the church, the village finally heard it.

It wasn't a cheer. It was the sound of a mountain grinding its teeth.

The back wall of the sanctuary didn't fall; it dissolved. The river, fed by the exploded spring beneath the altar and the main channel bursting its banks outside, hit the structure with the force of a battering ram.

Zion was small. That was the only reason he survived the first second.

The crush of the crowd shielded him from the debris. He was knocked sideways, slammed against the stone pillar he had been standing next to. The water hit his legs—cold, thick, and moving so fast it felt like solid concrete.

"Mama!" he screamed, but the sound was swallowed by the noise of timber snapping.

The church was no longer a building; it was a centrifuge. Pews, hymnals, hats, and people churned in a rising soup of muddy, churning water.

Zion saw Sister Etta. She was clinging to the back of a pew, her mouth open in a silent scream, before the pew twisted in the current and swept her out into the harsh glare of the afternoon through the gaping breach where the wall had dissolved.

"Grab the rail!"

A hand clamped onto the back of Zion's shirt. It was Marcia. She had hooked the crook of her cane over the iron railing of the side window, anchoring herself against the flood. With her other hand, she hauled Zion up out of the swirl.

"Where is she?" Zion choked, spitting mud.

Marcia pointed.

Caro was fighting. She hadn't been swept away, but she was pinned. A heavy oak beam from the roof had fallen across the aisle, trapping the hem of her skirt. The water was already at her waist. With the cutlass lost in the chaos, she clawed at the sodden fabric, desperately trying to rip herself free from the weight.

"Caro!" Marcia screamed.

The water rose another foot in a single surge. It wasn't just water—it was filled with glittering shards of glass. The millions of pieces of the broken jars were swirling in the flood like shrapnel.

Caro tore the last thread. She lunged toward them, wading through the chest-high current. She reached out, her fingers brushing Marcia's.

Marcia locked her hand around Caro's wrist—her own scar flashing white with the strain—and pulled.

They tumbled out the side window, landing in the mud of the churchyard just as the main steeple groaned, tilted, and collapsed inward into the nave.

"Up!" Caro gasped, dragging Zion to his feet. "We have to get high!"

The churchyard was gone. The ground they were standing on was already dissolving into slurry. The river had bypassed the bend; it was cutting a straight line through the village.

"The school roof!" Zion yelled.

The schoolhouse stood on a limestone ridge, the highest point in the valley besides the church. But between them and the school lay the road—and the road was now a rapid.

They didn't run; they stumbled, picking their way to the target. They didn't look back at the church. There was nothing to see but a heavy, heaving shape where the building used to be, sinking into the earth.

They reached the edge of the road. The water here was shin-deep but fast, carrying debris—fence posts, dead chickens, plastic crates.

Patch was there.

The dog was standing on a floating section of wooden fencing, barking frantically at the swirling, mud-choked current. He saw Zion and leaped into the water, paddling hard against the current to reach them.

"Come, boy!" Zion cried. He grabbed the dog by the scruff of the neck and hauled him onto the higher mud.

"Don't look down," Marcia warned, her voice tight.

Zion looked. He couldn't help it. The Stone in his pocket was humming, vibrating against his leg like a tuning fork. It wanted him to look.

The water rushing over his boots wasn't just brown mud. It was luminous with a faint, oily sheen. And in the swirls of the current, shapes were forming and dissolving.

A face, stretched long in the water—Etta's husband. A hand, reaching up from the foam—Auntie Myra's lost child.

The jars were broken, but the contents hadn't vanished. The memories, the secrets, the "shame" that Elias had bottled —it was all in the water now. The river was physically carrying the history of the village.

"They crying," Zion whispered, horrified.

"They are flowing," Marcia said, pushing him forward. "Move, Zion. If you stop to listen, you join them."

They scrambled up the limestone ridge, slipping on wet grass. The schoolhouse loomed ahead, a concrete block structure that looked solid.

They weren't the only ones.

Dozens of villagers were already there, clambering onto the flat zinc roof of the dining area. They were wet, muddied, and silent. The hysteria of the "Crusade" was gone. There was no singing now. No one was praising the miracle. They were shivering, huddled in groups, staring out at the end of their world.

Caro boosted Zion up the drainpipe. He scrambled onto the roof and reached down to pull her up. Marcia came last, leaving her cane behind in the mud because she needed both hands to climb.

They collapsed on the wet slick zinc roof.

From this height, they could see the valley.

The sun broke through the storm clouds. It illuminated the apocalypse. The village was gone. In its place was a wide, churning lake of copper silt that moved. The roofs of the houses poked up like islands. The tops of the mango trees were swaying in the current.

And in the center of the devastation, where the church had stood, there was a whirlpool—a massive, spinning vortex that was sucking everything down into the hollow where the jars had been. It was the drain of the world.

"The Pastor," Caro whispered, shivering violently. "You see him?"

Zion scanned the silt-choked water. He saw tree trunks. He saw the carcass of a goat. He saw the roof of the shop spinning slowly.

But he didn't see the man in the white suit.

"The water took him," Zion said. He felt The Stone in his pocket. It was vibrating so hard his leg went numb.

"No," Marcia said, pointing a shaking finger toward the whirlpool. "Look."

In the center of the spinning vortex, something white bobbed to the surface. It wasn't drifting. It was standing still, fighting the spin. It was Pastor Williams. He had found something to hold onto—maybe the top of the altar, or the cross itself. He was chest-deep in the center of the maelstrom, screaming at the water. He wasn't screaming for help. He was preaching.

Chapter 22
The Pastor's Baptism

From the roof of the schoolhouse, the devastation looked like a map drawn in black ink.

The valley of Clarendon, usually a patchwork of green cane and dust-brown roads, was gone. In its place was a single, heaving body of water that stretched from the hills to the horizon. It moved with a terrifying, muscular sluggishness, carrying whole trees, zinc roofs, and the bloated carcasses of livestock.

But the survivors on the roof were not looking at the horizon. They were looking at the whirlpool.

It spun directly over the site of the church foundation—a massive, rotating eye of dark water. It was the drain of the valley, sucking the flood down into the hollow where the jars had been.

And in the center of the eye, Pastor Williams was dying.

He had found a piece of the roof truss—a cross-section of timber that formed a rough 'X'. He clung to it, chest-deep in the center of the vortex.

Any other man would be screaming for a rope. But Thomas Williams was not in the river. In his mind, the water beating against his chest was the applause of the multitude. The roar of the flood was the stadium cheering his name.

"He's laughing," Zion whispered.

It was true. Even from this distance, they could see the Pastor's head thrown back. His white suit was gone, stripped away by the mud, leaving him in his undershirt, but he raised one hand to the sky in a gesture of benediction.

Debris circled him in the whirlpool—broken pews, clothing, the shattered remains of the pulpit.

In the clear light of day, they watched as he pointed to a dead goat spinning past him. He waved to a floating door as if it were a deacon.

"Welcome!" he shouted. "Welcome to the harvest!"

On the roof, the villagers huddled in silence. They were wet, shivering, and stripped of their judgment. Watching the Pastor's madness didn't feel like justice; it felt like looking into a grave.

Marcia moved to the edge of the parapet. She watched the whirlpool with cold, ancient eyes.

"Him don't see the water," she murmured. "He sees what he bought."

An old woman near them—Sister Agatha, who had lost her teeth years ago and rarely spoke—crossed herself. She stared at the way the water rose up around the Pastor, forming a high, slick wall that seemed to pause before crashing.

"Is not just water," Agatha whispered, her gums working nervously. "You see how it comb itself? Smooth like hair?"

Caro looked. The current was strange. It didn't chop or splash. It slid in long, glossy strands, winding around the Pastor, tightening the circle.

"River Mumma," Agatha breathed the name so low it was almost a thought. "The Old Mother come to clean her house."

"Hush, Agatha," Caro said sharply. "Don't call spirits now."

"She not a spirit," Marcia said, her voice hard. "She is the River. And she is taking back what was stolen."

In the center of the vortex, the timber gave way.

The Pastor slipped. The water rose to his chin.

And then, the sound changed.

The roar of the "Stadium"—the cheering multitude he had heard for twenty years—cut out. It didn't fade; it vanished, as if a wire had been cut.

The silence that rushed in was deafening. It was the silence of a dead valley.

Williams blinked. The golden light of the glory faded into the grey, muddy reality of the flood. He looked around.

He didn't see a choir. He saw dead livestock spinning in the muck. He saw the shattered remains of his pulpit drifting past like driftwood. He saw the villagers on the roof, looking down at him not with adoration, but with pity.

The Silver Jar was broken. The anesthesia was gone.

For the first time in twenty years, Thomas Williams saw exactly what he was.

"No," he whispered. It wasn't a prayer. It was a realization.

He looked down at the water. It wasn't the River Jordan. It was brown, heavy, and smelling of the grave he had dug for himself.

He opened his mouth to scream—not a sermon, but a plea for forgiveness.

But the River didn't want his apology. It wanted his silence.

The wall of water collapsed. The whirlpool accelerated. It didn't just pull him down; it embraced him.

The Pastor threw his arms up, his face twisted in a mask of absolute, lucid terror.

He went under.

There was no struggle. No thrashing. The water simply folded over his head like a heavy, wet sheet.

Gloop.

He was gone.

The timber cross popped back up a second later, empty.

The whirlpool spun for another minute, digesting. Then, slowly, the spin began to widen. The aggression left the immediate area. The water settled into a fast, flat current, rushing over the place where the church had been.

On the roof, no one moved. The background noise of the flood was still there—the noise Thomas heard as the noise of the Stadium—but the voice of the man who had summoned it was silenced.

"He's gone," Zion said.

He didn't sound sad. He sounded like a clock that had just struck the hour.

Marcia turned away from the edge. She sat down heavily on the slick zinc, leaning her head against her knees.

"The head of the snake is cut off," she said.

"But the body is still moving," Caro said, looking at the water lapping just a few feet below the roofline.

She was right. The Pastor was dead, but the river wasn't done. The water was still rising. It crept up the drainpipe, inch by inch, dark and hungry.

Zion walked to the edge. He looked down into the black flow. The Stone was burning his leg.

The Lady hadn't come for the Pastor. The Pastor was just debris.

She had come to retrieve The Stone she'd given, the Anchor. And she was climbing the stairs to get it.

CHAPTER 23
The High Ground

The roof was not a refuge; it was a drum.

The rain had returned, a hard, vertical downpour that hammered against the corrugated zinc sheets of the school's dining shed. The sound was deafening—a relentless, metallic roar that made conversation impossible.

There were forty people huddled on the flat, sloping metal. They clung to the nail heads and the ridge caps, slipping on the slick, rusting dull grey surface. Every time the building shuddered under the impact of a floating log, a collective gasp rippled through the group, lost in the noise of the storm.

Zion sat near the guttering, his knees pulled to his chest. Patch was curled tight against his side, shivering violently.

The dog wasn't looking at the people; he was staring fixedly at the churning flow rising inches below the eaves.

"It not stopping," a man shouted, cupping his hands to his neighbor's ear. "The water passing the window line!"

Caro crawled over the wet zinc to where Marcia sat. Marcia was staring out at the silt-choked lake that used to be the playground.

"The Pastor is gone," Caro yelled over the rain. "Why isn't it going down?"

Marcia wiped rain from her eyes. She looked like a statue carved from wood and grief.

"Because the debt isn't paid!" she shouted back. "Thomas was just the doorman! The river didn't come for him!"

She pointed to the debris piling up against the cinderblock walls of the school.

"It's looking!" Marcia said. "Can't you feel it? It's searching the house!"

She was right. The water wasn't just flowing past; it felt predatory. Eddies swirled around the corners of the building, testing the masonry. The current sucked at the doors, banging them open and shut in dull thuds, creating a slow hollow rhythm... a count down.

And the water was occupied.

The "Rot" that had plagued the village for weeks—the mold, the secrets, the shame—was now swimming.

Zion saw it first. He looked over the edge of the gutter.

In the dark wash below, the shards of the broken jars glittered like underwater stars. But mixed with the glass were shapes that made his stomach turn.

He saw a wedding veil floating like a jellyfish—Etta's daughter's shame. He saw a ledger book, pages dissolving—The shopkeeper's stolen accounts.

The villagers saw them too.

"Lord have mercy," Sister Agatha whimpered, pointing at a swirl of foam that looked uncannily like the face of her dead husband. "It bringin' everything back."

The survivors shrank away from the edge. They huddled in the center of the roof, terrified not just of drowning, but of being touched by the water. The flood was a mirror, and it was showing them everything they had paid Elias to hide.

Zion felt a heat on his thigh.

It started as a warmth, then turned into a burning throb. The Stone.

He tried to ignore it. He pressed his hand over his pocket, trying to smother the sensation. But the vibration traveled up his arm, into his neck, into his teeth.

Thump. Thump. Thump.

It matched the rhythm of the water slapping against the walls.

The Stone pulled.

It wasn't a metaphor. Zion felt a physical force, like a magnet, dragging his body toward the edge of the roof. He dug his boots into the ridges of the zinc. He grabbed a nail head.

"Zion?" Caro saw him struggling. She lunged forward, grabbing his pants waist. "What wrong with you? Sit still!"

Zion looked at her. His eyes were wide, the pupils blown black.

"She knows I have it," he whispered. The voice was the Strange Tongue—hollow and absolute.

"Who?" Caro cried, terrified by the look on his face.

"The Lady," the voice answered. Zion looked at the water. "She is cleaning the house to find the key. If I don't give it to her... she's going to knock the house down."

As if in answer, the schoolhouse groaned.

A massive tree trunk, propelled by the main current, slammed into the corner of the dining shed.

CRUNCH.

The zinc roof buckled. A seam popped open with a sound like a gunshot, slicing through the rain noise. The entire structure leaned three inches to the right.

Screams erupted. People slid down the slick metal, clawing for purchase.

"The walls giving way!" a man yelled.

Zion let go of the nail.

He stood up. The wind whipped his wet shirt against his ribs. He leaned slightly into the wind, maintaining his balance, his eyes squinting as he struggled to see. On the slippery, angled roof, he stood perfectly balanced, anchored by the weight in his pocket.

"Zion, get down!" Caro screamed, reaching for him.

He stepped out of her reach. He walked down the slope of the roof, toward the gutter, toward the dark, churning water.

Patch stood up too. The dog didn't bark. He walked beside the boy, his tail low, his eyes fixed on the darkness beyond the edge.

"She not looking for the village," Zion said, his voice carrying strangely over the storm. "She looking for her heart."

He reached the edge. The water was right there, lapping under the overhang of the zinc roof.

Zion didn't jump. He just stood there, a small figure in the rain, offering himself to the flood.

And then, the water noticed him.

The swirling debris stopped. The current shifted. The waves that had been battering the walls suddenly smoothed out.

A silence fell over the immediate area, heavy and thick.

Out in the darkness of the playground, the water began to rise up. Not a wave. A shape.

The Lady was here.

CHAPTER 24
The Lady's Shape

The rain stopped.

It didn't taper off; it was cut. One second the storm was hammering the zinc roof, and the next, the air was dead silent.

The silence was worse than the roar.

On the roof of the dining shed, the survivors froze. The sudden quiet pressed against their ears. The only sound left was the slap, slap, slap of the black water against the aluminum guttering, inches below their feet.

Zion stood at the edge. The wind had died, leaving his wet shirt clinging to his ribs. He didn't look back at his mother. He looked into the silt-choked flow.

"She's here," he whispered.

Out in the flooded playground, the water began to bulge.

It wasn't a wave. It was a displacement. Something massive was rising from the deep, pushing the floodwaters up in a smooth, dark hill.

It didn't have eyes. It didn't have a mouth. It was a column of rotating water, thick with mud and silt, rising twenty feet into the air. It held its shape against gravity, a liquid tower that blotted out the remaining light.

The villagers scrambled back toward the ridge of the roof, whimpering. Sister Agatha buried her face in her hands.

"River Mumma," she prayed, her voice shaking. "Golden Comb. Old Mother. Mercy."

The shape shifted. It leaned toward the schoolhouse. It wasn't a woman, yet the suggestion was there—the curve of a shoulder made of foam, the tilt of a head made of shadow.

It was vast. It was indifferent. It was the heavy, wet earth waking up to reclaim its bed.

The Tower of Water loomed over the roof. It cast a cold, damp shadow over Zion. Its immense liquid mass absorbed the bruised afternoon light, plunging the survivors into a sudden, spiritual darkness.

Caro lunged forward. "Zion! Get back!"

She grabbed for his arm, but Marcia caught her.

"Don't touch him," Marcia hissed, holding Caro back with surprising strength. "He is the only thing keeping the roof dry. Look."

Caro looked. The water was lapping right at the soles of Zion's boots, but it didn't rise further. The Entity was waiting.

Zion stood trembling. The Stone in his pocket was burning with an intense heat; he could smell the fabric of his shorts scorching, yet the skin beneath felt only a fierce tingling warmth that refused to blister.

He opened his mouth. The voice that came out was the Strange Tongue—the voice of the Prosecutor, the voice of The Stone.

"RETURN," Zion said.

It wasn't a question. He wasn't speaking to the Lady; he was translating for her.

The water tower rippled. A spray of mist hit the roof, smelling of ancient mud and iron.

THE COVENANT OF GLASS

"THE CORK IS OUT," Zion intoned, his eyes rolling back, showing the whites. "THE CONTRACT IS VOID. RETURN THE WEIGHT."

"Give it to her!" a man shouted from the back of the roof. "Whatever you have, boy, give it to her!"

"He can't just throw it!" Marcia shouted back, her voice cracking. "It's an Anchor! If he drops it wrong, the wave will crush us!"

Zion reached into his pocket. His hand shook violently. Strangely, the salt was dry but the boy did not notice. He pulled out the black stone.

In the presence of the Lady, The Stone changed. It was no longer dull. It pulsed with a wet, black light, sucking the shadows into it. It hummed with a sound like a heavy drumbeat.

Thrum. Thrum. Thrum.

The Lady—the massive water shape—leaned closer. The "face" of the wave was only feet from Zion. He could see the debris suspended in her body: the silver shards of the Judas jar, the pages of the Bible, the white fabric of the Pastor's suit.

She was made of their destruction.

Zion looked at The Stone. Then he looked at the water.

He understood.

He turned his head slightly, just enough to see Caro out of the corner of his eye. The Strange Tongue faded, replaced by the terrified voice of a twelve-year-old boy.

"Mama," he whispered. "She come for it."

"Zion, no," Caro wept, reaching out.

"I have to give it back," he said, his voice breaking. "It's the only way to make her stop."

He didn't throw The Stone. That would be an insult.

She had come to retrieve The Stone she'd given, the Anchor. And she was climbing the stairs to get it.

He stepped forward.

One step. Two steps.

He stepped off the edge of the zinc roof, into the air, and let the darkness take him.

"ZION!"

Caro's scream tore the night in half.

Patch barked—a single, sharp command—and leaped after him.

Boy, dog, and stone hit the black water together. They didn't splash. They vanished instantly, swallowed by the throat of the river.

The water tower shuddered. It hung in the air for one terrible second, defying natural laws before silently receding, covering the boy and the dog.

Chapter 25

The Choice of The Stone

The world turned upside down.

One moment, there was rain and wind and the scream of his mother. The next, there was only the crushing, silent weight of the River.

Zion didn't swim. He couldn't. The Stone in his pocket was no longer an anchor; it was a millstone. It dragged him down with terrifying speed, piercing the skin of the flood and plummeting toward the deep.

The water was black, but Zion could see.

It was the "Strange Sight" again. The muddy water appeared to him as a thick, swirling amber fog. He saw the suspended debris of the village hanging in the void—a chair, a chicken coop, the Pastor's white shoe—all drifting in slow motion.

He felt a furred body brush against his leg. Patch. The dog was paddling fiercely, diving with him, refusing to break the bond.

The current caught them. They weren't just sinking; they were being sucked into the throat of the whirlpool.

Zion spun. The pressure built in his ears. He felt the water twisting him, preparing to grind him against the debris of the church.

But The Stone protected him. It created a small, heavy sphere of stillness around his body. The debris bounced off an invisible shield. He was the eye of the storm.

He hit the bottom.

It wasn't mud. It was concrete.

He was standing on the ruined foundation of the church. The walls were gone, the pews were gone, but the slab remained. And in the center, where the altar used to be, the earth had opened up.

The "Nest"—the hollow where the jars had been—was glowing. Not with fire, but with a cold, blue phosphorescence. The source of the river.

She was waiting.

For a fleeting second, Zion saw the shape she took when they first met. Her features seemed to shift like foam on water, and her eyes were hollows of dark liquid. As she raised her hand to beckon him closer, the image dissolved immediately, morphing through the towering woman of foam he remembered from the roof. Down here, she was not foam or shadow; she was just a presence—a vast, heavy consciousness that filled the crushing dark. She rippled through the water, cold and ancient.

Zion saw her clearly. She wasn't angry. She was just... empty. She was a house with the door blown off.

She hovered over the glowing hole in the earth. She was waiting for the door to be shut.

The weight, the water whispered in his head. Give me the weight.

THE COVENANT OF GLASS

Zion reached into his pocket. His lungs were burning now. The air he had taken on the roof was gone. The darkness was creeping into the edges of his vision.

He pulled out The Stone.

It was heavy. Impossibly heavy. It felt like he was holding a mountain in his small hand.

He looked at the hole in the foundation. The water spewing out of it was violent, raging, chaotic. It was the chaos that had killed the Pastor.

Zion stepped forward. He forced his hand down against the pressure of the uprising current.

He didn't throw it.

He knelt.

With the last of his strength, he placed the black stone into the center of the glowing blue hole.

It didn't make a splash. It made a sound like a lock tumbling shut.

Thud.

The Stone seated itself.

Instantaneously, the violence stopped.

The glowing blue light snapped off. The roar in Zion's ears vanished. The "pull" of the whirlpool died.

Gravity returned to the world.

The water was no longer a monster; it was just water. Heavy, cold, and still.

Zion's lungs spasmed. He opened his mouth to scream for air, but only bubbles came out. The darkness rushed in to take him.

He felt a rough snout nudge his face.

Then, a force—not the Lady, but the natural buoyancy of the water—lifted him. He floated up, limp and small, rising toward the surface of the new, quiet lake.

~ ~ ~

Caro was screaming his name on the roof, her voice raw and broken.

"Zion! ZION!"

The floodwaters below were dark and still. The terrifying whirlpool had vanished as if a plug had been pulled. The water swirled lazily, choked with debris, but the aggression was gone.

"Him gone," Marcia whispered, staring at the black glass of the water. "He paid the debt."

"No!" Caro shrieked. She tried to slide down the roof, to jump in after him.

"Caro, stop!" Marcia grabbed her. "You can't save him from the deep!"

Then, a splash.

Thirty feet away, the head of a dog broke the surface.

Patch.

The dog paddled frantically, coughing water, shaking his ears. He wasn't swimming to the roof. He was paddling in a tight circle, whining.

He dipped his head under, grabbed something, and pulled.

A small arm flopped onto a floating piece of the church ceiling.

"Zion!"

Caro slid down the zinc roof, ignoring the danger. She hit the water and swam. She had never swum so fast in her life. She reached the debris.

He was pale. His lips were blue. He wasn't breathing.

Caro hauled him onto the floating wood. She pounded on his back. "Breathe! Breathe, baby, breathe!"

Nothing.

She pressed her mouth to his. She forced her own breath into his lungs. She pushed on his small chest.

"Come back," she sobbed. "You answered once. You answered the river. Now answer me!"

Patch licked the boy's ear, whining low in his throat.

Zion's chest hitched.

A spasm wracked his body. He rolled onto his side and vomited river water. He gasped—a long, ragged, tearing sound—and sucked in the night air.

Caro collapsed over him, weeping, holding him so tight she might break his ribs.

Zion blinked. His eyes were dark brown again. The "old" look was gone. The Strange Tongue was gone. He was just a twelve-year-old boy, cold and wet and scared.

He looked at the water. It was calm. It lapped gently against the wood, quiet as a sleeping child.

"It's done, Mama," he whispered. "The door shut."

CHAPTER 26
The Receding

The sun did not rise; it leaked into the valley.

It was a grey, sickly dawn. The rain had stopped hours ago, and the silence that hung over the schoolhouse roof was heavy and wet.

The water was leaving.

It didn't drain like a bathtub; it rushed. The River, having reclaimed its debt, was retreating to its bed with violent speed. It dragged the wreckage of the village with it—trees, zinc sheets, dead livestock, and the unrecognizable ruin of the church—all sucking toward the ocean.

Zion sat on the edge of the roof, wrapped in a tablecloth someone had found in the cafeteria. He was shivering, but his eyes were clear. Beside him, Patch slept the sleep of the dead, his fur drying into stiff spikes.

"It going down fast," Marcia said. She was standing at the parapet, looking down.

The mud was visible now. Thick, black silt covered everything like a shroud. The village looked like it had been dipped in tar.

"We have to go down," Zion said.

"Not yet," Caro said, touching his shoulder. "It's too deep."

"No," Zion said. He stood up. The Strange Tongue was gone, but a new, quiet certainty had taken its place. "He is waiting."

They climbed down the drainpipe when the mud was still knee-deep. It was hard going. The silt was slick and treacherous, hiding holes and sharp debris.

They didn't go to their house. They went to the foundation.

The church was erased. The stone walls were gone. Only the concrete slab remained, cracked down the middle. The guango tree had been uprooted, lying on its side like a fallen giant.

And clinging to the roots of the tree, half-buried in the muck, was a shape.

It wasn't a man. It was the residue of one. The shadow of Elias, shattered and dispersed by the explosion in the church, had washed down here and curdled back into a mass. It was grey, translucent, and shivering, like oil trying to separate itself from the mud.

Elias.

The blast had stripped him of his power, shattered his jars, and left him naked. He was no longer the terrifying obeah man of the cane fields. He was just a stain on the landscape.

He looked up as Zion approached. His single eye was wide with a primal terror.

"Boy," Elias wheezed. His voice sounded like wind blowing through dry grass. "Help me. It pulls."

Zion stopped five feet away. Patch growled low in his throat.

"The Anchor is back," Zion said.

"I can teach you," Elias begged, his hands clawing at the mud. "You have the sight now. You hear the voices. I can show you how to rule them."

Marcia limped forward, her cane lost in the flood, looking down at the creature that had owned her for twenty years.

"He doesn't want to rule," Marcia said. "He wants to live."

Elias sneered at her, a flash of his old malice returning. "You think you are free, Marcia? You carry my mark. You are mine."

"I carry a scar," Marcia corrected. "But the book is closed."

The mud beneath Elias began to bubble.

It wasn't heat. It was liquefaction. The silt was turning into quicksand.

"No!" Elias shrieked. He tried to pull his legs free, but the earth was hungry. "I made a deal! I kept the order!"

"You stole her heart," Zion said softly. "Now you belong to her."

The Lady didn't manifest as a giant water spirit this time. She didn't need to. She was the mud. She was the gravity.

The ground opened.

Elias clawed at the roots of the guango tree, his fingers passing through the wood like smoke. He wasn't being washed out to sea. He was being dragged under. Down into the cold, dark geology of the riverbed, to be pressed between layers of rock and time.

"Thomas!" he screamed, calling for his servant who was already gone. "THOMAS!"

The mud folded over his head.

There was a wet, sucking sound. Then silence.

The shadow was gone. The stain was washed clean.

~ ~ ~

"Mama."

Zion wasn't looking at the spot where Elias had vanished. He was looking toward the treeline, where the path from the hills came down to the river.

A figure was walking through the mud.

He moved slowly, stumbling, as if his legs had forgotten the shape of flat ground. He was thin, his skin gray and bleached like a root pulled from deep soil. He wore rags that were caked with a heavy, gray clay that smelled of sulfur.

Caro knew the walk.

She didn't breathe. She didn't move. She couldn't let herself hope, because hope felt more dangerous than the flood.

The man stopped at the edge of the clearing. He looked at the ruined church. He looked at the vast, mud-slicked valley. He raised a hand, rubbing his eyes as if the sunlight hurt them.

"Caro?"

It was a voice unused to speaking—cracked, dry, and hesitant.

Caro made a sound that wasn't a word. It was a sob that tore its way out of her chest. She ran. She slipped in the mud, scrambled up, and ran again. She hit him with enough force to knock him back a step.

Samuel caught her. He was solid. He was warm. He smelled of damp earth and thirteen years of lost time, but he was real.

"Thank you, Jesus," he whispered into her hair, his voice trembling. "I've found her… I've found you, Caro!" Tears streamed from his eyes.

He pulled back to look at her, his eyes wide with the shock of waking up. Then he embraced her again, thirteen years of pent-up longing found release.

"I was close," he whispered into her hair, his voice trembling. "For years, I was in the dark, trapped. I could hear the water... but I couldn't put the shovel down."

"Then I heard glass break," he said. "I heard a crash... and things changed. It felt like my hands were free again, no longer chained to the shovel, yet there was never any chain."

He gestured vaguely toward the river, his voice shaking.

"The surge took me, Caro. It washed me out of the sinkhole like a leaf. I rode the flood, clinging to a log. I thought I was dead... until I washed up about a mile from here."

He looked at her, the recognition finally absolute.

"Then it all came back. I remembered… I remembered everything. I remembered when I left you I promised to return after my trip, but I never did. I couldn't. I was trapped."

Caro watched him as he poured out his words, relief and disbelief all rolled into one. She didn't have the words; she just wanted to devour his presence, so she let him speak. But then the full reality of the moment struck her.

Caro stepped back, clutching his hands tightly. "Wait," she choked out, tears still streaming. She pulled Zion forward, who stood quietly watching them. "Samuel, look at me. Look at him."

Samuel's eyes, still clouded by shock, settled on Zion. He looked at the boy's face, then back at Caro, hope and confusion creasing his brow.

"This is Zion," Caro whispered, her voice raw with pride and pain. "Your son. He's the one who brought you home."

Samuel stared, recognition dawning slow and absolute. He knelt in the thick mud and simply held out one trembling, clawed hand to the boy.

"My son," Samuel breathed, his voice thick.

Marcia watched the reunion silently before speaking.

"It was one of the jars with the blue wax," she said, nodding at the reunited couple. "That was the one holding his will and blocking his memories. As long as it was sealed, he could only live in the moment; he had to obey. Breaking the glass set him free."

"This is Marcia," Caro interjected. "We have a lot to catch up on."

Marcia noticed his hands were permanently curled, the fingers hooked and calloused thick as leather, as if they had molded around a handle that was never put down.

"Where were you?" she asked, stepping closer. Her voice was sharp, cutting through the emotion. She was looking at his hands with the dawn of horrific understanding. "You weren't just kept, Samuel. You were used."

Samuel looked down at his clawed hands. He flexed them painfully.

"The Throat," Samuel whispered. "I was in the Swallow's Throat."

Zion frowned. "The sinkhole? Up past the Black Cane?"

"It was blocked," Samuel rasped. "The river... she kept bringing logs, mud, stones. She wanted to come up. She wanted to flood the basin."

He rubbed his shoulder, wincing at a phantom weight.

"I had to keep it clear. If I stopped, the water rose. I dug for thirteen years to keep the water underground."

"Alone?" Caro asked, horrified. "One man held back the river?"

Samuel shook his head slowly.

"Not at the start," he said. "There were three of us. Bigga was there when I got there, then a boy from Morgan's Pass named Leopold came a few years after. We worked the line together."

He looked at the mud, his eyes dark with memory.

"The river took Bigga in a flood after we cleared a jam. A log broke his back. And Leopold... Leopold just stopped moving four years ago. He fell down in the mud and never got up."

"And Elias didn't replace them?" Marcia asked, her eyes narrowing.

"No," Samuel said. "He came to the edge of the pit and looked at us. He looked... tired. He just pointed at me and said, 'Dig faster, keep the throat clear.' So I did. For four years, I dug for three men."

Marcia struck the mud with her foot, a grim satisfaction on her face.

"He was too weak," she said. "Binding a new soul takes strength he didn't have anymore. He was spending every drop of blood just to keep the glass from cracking. He was holding the Pastor, holding me, holding the dam—and who knows how many more poor souls."

She looked at the ruins of the church, then at Samuel.

"He split the river," Marcia said, piecing the architecture together. "The Pastor was the Cork—he held the Spirit down so she couldn't rise."

She gestured to Samuel's ruined hands.

"And you were the Dredge. You kept the throat clear to suppress the natural cycle, forcing the water underground."

Zion looked at the river.

It was no longer forced into the narrow throat of the sinkhole—a place of natural flow that was interrupted at times by blockages that spilled over the banks, washing into the low basins that Elias had starved for twenty years. Those were the swamps that Elias had to keep dry for the syndicate and their sugar plantation. The water moved with a living rhythm now—finding its natural pattern, feeding the land then fleeing it. A natural cycle. It found its balance.

Something white moved in the fresh silt. A bird with long, spindly legs picked its way through the mud, stepping delicately among the reeds.

Zion tugged on his mother's sleeve. "Mama? What is that?"

Caro followed his gaze. Her eyes widened, soft with a memory she hadn't touched since she was a girl.

"That is a heron, Zion," she whispered, a smile breaking through her exhaustion. "They used to live here, before the cane took the water. They only come where the land is breathing."

Samuel rested his hand on Zion's shoulder, looking at the bird.

"The marsh is coming back," Samuel said quietly. "The silence is over."

Zion looked at the water, then at his father's hands, finally at rest.

"The work is done," Zion whispered, watching the bird hunt. "The river is free."

Old Man Zion—The Keeper of the Flow

The boy rolled the black marble again. "And Elias? What happened to him?"

The old man stopped rocking. He looked toward the river, where the sun was setting in a bruise of purple and gold.

"Elias forgot the first rule of the water," the old man said. "He thought the river was a thing he could own. He knew the river had its own mind, but he wanted to control it."

"You mean River Mumma?"

"We don't say that name too loud," the old man warned, though his eyes crinkled with amusement. "Let's just say The Lady. But yes. He stole from her."

"What did he steal?"

The old man held out his hand, cupping it as if holding water.

"Think of the river like a living body. It has blood, and it has a pulse. The Stone... The Stone was the Heart. It was the Regulator. It told the water when to rush and when to rest. It kept the balance."

The boy frowned, trying to picture it. "So Elias cut out the heart?"

"He dug it out," the old man nodded. "Because he wanted the land for himself. He wanted dry fields for his cane and a dry yard for his power. But you can't just take the heart out of a thing and expect it to behave. The river went wild."

The old man made a fist.

"So, to stop the river from washing him away, Elias built a Dam. He didn't use concrete. He used glass. He filled that empty hole in the foundation under the church with the Jars

—bottles full of debts and secrets. He plugged the wound with other people's sins."

"Like a cork?" Tariq asked.

"Like a wall," Zion corrected. "But here is the trouble with walls made of magic, Tariq. They are heavy. They need a strong foundation to keep them from cracking under the pressure."

Zion tapped the arm of his chair.

"Elias had to pour his own life into the mortar to keep the glass from shattering. That was the trap he didn't see. He became the Watchman at the Gate. As long as that wall stood, he was chained to it. He spent twenty years in a cage he built himself."

"Until it broke," the boy whispered.

"Until it broke," the old man agreed, a grim smile touching his lips. "And that was the trick, Tariq. That was the joke the river played on him."

Zion leaned forward, his milky eyes catching the last of the light.

"When the Pastor smashed that silver jar, the contract snapped. The invisible chain that held Elias to the cane fields was gone. In that split second, he was free. He wasn't the Watchman anymore. He could have walked away."

"So why didn't he?"

"Because he was standing in the path of the flood he had held back for twenty years," Zion said softly. "The breaking of the glass gave him his freedom and his death in the same breath. He didn't have time to run. The water doesn't negotiate with the man who stole its heart."

"But you fixed it."

"I didn't fix the wall," Zion said softly. "I gave it back its Heart. I put The Stone back in the socket."

He looked at the darkening sky, his milky eyes reflecting the first stars.

"And once the river had its Heart back, Tariq, it didn't need to fight anymore. It remembered its rhythm. It remembered balance and gravity. It stopped trying to drown the mountain and just went home to its bed."

"And Elias?"

"Elias was the architect of the obstruction," the old man said, his voice dropping to a rasp. "And when the flow started again... he was washed into the mud. She planted him."

"Planted him?"

"Deep," the old man said. "Under the marl. Under the rock. They say if you go down to the old foundation when the river is low, and you put your ear to the mud, you can hear him."

"What does he say?" the boy whispered, leaning in.

The old man chuckled, a dry, raspy sound.

"Nothing, Tariq. He doesn't have a mouth anymore. He is just part of the riverbed now. He is a stone for the water to walk on."

The old man reached into his pocket. For a second, his hand trembled, as if he expected to find something heavy there. But he pulled out a piece of hard candy wrapped in red paper.

"Here," he said, tossing it to the boy. "Sweetness for the living."

"And for the dead?" the boy asked, unwrapping it.

The old man looked at the darkening sky, where the first stars were appearing over the Peace River.

"For the dead," Zion said, "we give silence. And we give respect."

He closed his eyes, listening to the river flow in the distance—heavy, constant, and finally, finally free.

THE END

INSIDE THE COVENANT OF GLASS

BEHIND THE VEIL: The Roots of the Covenant
While The Covenant of Glass is a work of fiction, the shadow that hangs over the valley of Wataside is real.

Obeah and "The Science"
In Jamaican history, Obeah names a range of African-derived spiritual practices—healing, protection, divination, and spiritual attack—passed on through oral teaching, family lines, and village specialists, using herbs, baths, charms, prayers, and spirit work rather than formal manuals. By the early to mid-20th century, a distinct stream of practice grew around imported occult books from the Chicago publisher De Laurence, Scott & Co., especially grimoires like The Sixth and Seventh Books of Moses, which laid out magic in a structured, "textbook" form with seals, psalms, and set rituals. As

colonial authorities moved to restrict these books under customs rules tied to anti-Obeah policy, they circulated clandestinely and came to signify a more book-learned, systematized approach to power; practitioners who relied on De Laurence texts were said to be working "The Science," in contrast to older, orally transmitted Obeah, and were regarded as having a more academic or technical command of spiritual force.

Elias is a fictional echo of that era—a man who sought to turn that spiritual fear into a physical weapon.

The "De Laurence" Prohibition

The "Science" referenced in the novel draws directly on this history. De Laurence publications, though produced in the United States, became deeply entangled with Jamaican Obeah, to the point that authorities specifically targeted them for prohibition as part of the wider effort to police spirit work and "superstitious" practices. The legal focus fell especially on the importation and circulation of these books, which were treated as dangerous amplifiers of an already-feared spiritual underground.

THE COVENANT OF GLASS

The Symbolism of Blue

The significance of "Blue" in the novel's "Blue Wax" builds on the widespread use of blue in Afro-Caribbean protective traditions. Across the region, blue paints and dyes—along with commercial laundry bluing products—often simply called "Blue"—have been used on doors and windows, in baths and house-washing, or applied to the body as forms of spiritual defense. In many communities, blue is understood to confuse, "blind," or repel malevolent forces, turning ordinary domestic materials into quiet wards that mark the boundary between the vulnerable human body and an unseen, spiritually charged world.

Beyond the Glass

The "Science" of Wataside operates on a logic of debt and displacement—a rigid system where every jar represents a stolen memory and every flood is a calculated return of energy. While the story of Zion and Caro has reached its end, the blueprints of Elias's dam and the laws of the "Single Seal" remain for those who wish to understand the mechanics of the Covenant. If you seek to know how a river was silenced for twenty years, and what truly happened to the souls trapped in the foundation, we invite you to consult the full Grimoire.

EXPLORE THE MAGIC

1. The Fictional Mechanics

How did Elias's specific magic work? Why did the jars hold the river? How did the "Law of the Single Seal" function? Visit the Grimoire of Wataside to unlock the deep lore and hidden rules of the novel.

[**Scan QR Code** or **Visit: https://fiwiroots.com/covenant-of-glass/secrets/**]

2. The Island's Culture and History

The Covenant of Glass is fiction, but the heritage is real. The Fiwi Roots Project is a comprehensive digital initiative dedicated to preserving the broad history, culture, and folklore of Jamaica. From the herbal wisdom of the Bush Doctor to the sweeping events of the Timeline and the geological reality of Physical Jamaica, we invite you to explore the full scope of the island's identity.

[**Scan QR Code** or **Visit: https://fiwiroots.com/**]

ABOUT THE AUTHOR

GLEN CARTY is an author who has dedicated years to researching and preserving the rich history and culture of Jamaica. His extensive documentation of the island's timeline —from its original people, the Tainos, to the diversity of those who came later; from its Great Houses to its influence on the world stage—forms the backbone of his storytelling and contributes to the broader educational mission of The Fiwi Roots Project.

He is a passionate advocate for the Young Dreamers Scholarship, a fund that provides financial support to students entering high school in Jamaica's deep rural interior. All royalties from his books published by Fiwi Roots Publishing go directly to the scholarship, investing in the very communities where stories like The Covenant of Glass are born.

His fiction is born from a fascination with this heritage, blending historical reality with the captivating, sometimes terrifying oral traditions of the Caribbean.

ALSO BY GLEN CARTY

THE SECRET PACT

Historical Fiction

Set in the aftermath of the First Maroon War, The Secret Pact is a gripping tale of rebellion, espionage, and a fragile peace. Readers have called it "unputdownable" and "a page-turner that reads like a spy thriller."

THE TIMELINE OF JAMAICA

Non-Fiction / Reference

A comprehensive guide to the events, people, and industries that shaped the island's identity. It was the research for this timeline that led to the creation of the Jamaica Timeline website and unearthed the fascinating stories that inspired his subsequent books—including The Covenant of

THE COVENANT OF GLASS

Glass, which leans into the cultural and folkloric tales of the island.

A NOTE TO THE READER

Independent authors live and die by word of mouth. If The Covenant of Glass kept you up at night, please consider leaving a short review on Amazon or Goodreads.

Even a single sentence helps other readers find the path to the river.